Look what people are saying about these talented authors...

Rhonda Nelson

"A home-run read. No filler here, just straight charm, chemistry and sex, all wrapped up and delivered with a bow."
—*RT Book Reviews* on *Merry Christmas, Baby*

"Well plotted and wickedly sexy, this one's got it all—including a completely scrumptious hero. A keeper."
—*RT Book Reviews* on *The Ranger*

"Totally entertaining, emotionally satisfying and very sexy, this is a super-strong book!"
—*RT Book Reviews* on *Blazing Bedtime Stories*

Tawny Weber

"Forget the hot chocolate, the wool socks and the space heater—Tawny Weber's *Sex, Lies and Mistletoe* will keep you plenty warm this season!"
—*USA TODAY*

"A sexy, sizzling, oh my God!, laugh out loud read. A must add to your Christmas romance book reading list."
—*Romancing the Rakes* about *Sex, Lies and Mistletoe*

"This is definitely not a story for the prim and proper."
—*Top Romance Novels* regarding *Breaking the Rules*

ABOUT THE AUTHORS

A Waldenbooks bestselling author, two-time RITA® Award nominee, *RT Book Reviews* Reviewers' Choice nominee and National Readers' Choice Award winner, **Rhonda Nelson** has more than thirty-five published books to her credit and many more coming down the pike. Rhonda and her family make their chaotic but happy home in a small town in northern Alabama. She loves to hear from her readers, so be sure to check her out at www.readRhondaNelson.com, follow her on Twitter @RhondaRNelson and like her on Facebook.

Avid reader, neurotic writer and die-hard shoe fanatic, **Tawny Weber** has been writing sassy, sexy stories for Harlequin Blaze since her first book hit the shelves in 2007. When not obsessing over deadlines, she's watching Johnny Depp movies, scrapbooking or hanging out on Facebook and Twitter. Come by and visit her on the web at www.tawnyweber.com.

Rhonda Nelson
Tawny Weber

BLAZING BEDTIME STORIES, VOLUME VII

TORONTO NEW YORK LONDON
AMSTERDAM PARIS SYDNEY HAMBURG
STOCKHOLM ATHENS TOKYO MILAN MADRID
PRAGUE WARSAW BUDAPEST AUCKLAND

ISBN-13: 978-0-373-79692-2

BLAZING BEDTIME STORIES, VOLUME VII

Copyright © 2012 by Harlequin Books S.A.

The publisher acknowledges the copyright holders
of the individual works as follows:

THE STEADFAST HOT SOLDIER
Copyright © 2012 by Rhonda Nelson

WILD THING
Copyright © 2012 by Tawny Weber

Recycling programs
for this product may
not exist in your area.

CONTENTS

RHONDA NELSON

THE STEADFAST HOT SOLDIER

For Brenda, rock star editor extraordinaire,
who always knows how to get the best out of me,
and for Tawny, my incredibly talented
and cool book-mate. Y'all are awesome.

1

Major John "Bear" Midwinter saw the Hydrangea, Mississippi, city limits sign swiftly approaching and thought the Seventh Circle of Hell might be a better name. His lips twitched with a pale effort at humor.

He supposed it didn't have the same cachet.

Hydrangea sounded picturesque, quaint and homey, and he supposed, to most of the residents who lived here—or ever had, for that matter—that's exactly the kind of town it was. He grimaced.

His fondest memory of Hydrangea, however, was leaving it.

True to its flowery namesake, dozens of multicolored blooms spilled off the bushes along either side of the road and, though he hadn't been near the town square in years, he knew the snowball-size flowers would be planted all around the white gazebo in its center. They'd be hanging from the lampposts in fancy planters, coaxed up trellises and displayed in wreaths on storefront doors. As a boy he'd ridden his bike on the sidewalks, stopped for strawberry milk shakes at Malone's Diner and sweet-talked chocolate stars from Ella Johnston, who ran the candy counter at the dry goods store.

It wasn't that he didn't have any good memories of Hydrangea—he did. But they had been few and far between.

As a U.S. Army Ranger and part of a Special Forces unit that specialized in hand-to-hand combat, Bear knew a thousand different ways to incapacitate, wound or kill an opponent. He could size up an adversary in the blink of an eye then isolate a weakness and use it to his advantage in another blink. He was supremely confident in his abilities. Some men, he'd been taught, were natural warriors and between his size—which was notable—and inherent skill, he knew he fell into that category. He was good at his job, confident in his ability to carry out his duties for Uncle Sam. He frowned.

But the duty he was facing here was another matter altogether.

Could he competently ready his mother's dance studio and apartment for the impending sale? Certainly. He wasn't a carpenter, but knew his way around a hammer well enough to handle the repairs. The better question—the one that had been circling the brain drain for weeks now—was why in the hell had he agreed to do them? What on earth had possessed him to agree to help her? Despite the fact that she was his mother, he certainly didn't owe her anything.

Duty, Bear thought. It was a bitch to shake, deserved or not.

Celeste Midwinter's parenting style had been more Mommy Dearest than June Cleaver. The day he'd walked out her door to go to college had been one of the happiest in his life. Until he'd moved out, there hadn't been a single day in his memory that she hadn't reminded him of how he'd ruined her life, ruined her body, ruined her career. A gifted ballet dancer, his mother had been living in New York, on the verge of stardom when she'd gotten pregnant with him. Her strict Catholic upbringing hadn't prevented her from having premarital sex, but it had kept her from aborting him.

He knew beyond a shadow of a doubt that she regretted it. He'd heard it from her own lips.

So why was he here? Why wasn't he using his leave to go on a real much-deserved vacation? Why hadn't he booked a trip to the beach? Taken a short cruise? Gone to Jamaica with his friends?

Other than some misguided sense of misplaced duty—there it was again, his downfall—and an odd, unexplainable expectation, he didn't have any idea.

He supposed, to some degree, he felt sorry for her. When her dancing career had ended and no help from his father had been forthcoming—Bear didn't even know the man's name and had certainly never met him—Celeste had literally thrown a dart at the map and relocated. Her family had disowned her as a result of the pregnancy, so she'd had no one to turn to, in what he knew had to be a very difficult time. She'd survived. She'd worked hard, built the studio up and into a business that had supported them and for that reason alone, if for no other, he hadn't been able to say no. His mother was hard, and whatever negligible maternal instincts she might have possessed had been poisoned by bitterness. But at the end of the day…she was the only family he had.

Who knew? Bear thought. Perhaps they'd be able to repair some of the damage over the next few days. He'd seen her less than half a dozen times over the last dozen years. He was certainly a different person. It was possible that she could be, too. That maybe, with age, had come a heavy dose of wisdom and a little bit of regret.

Bear made the turn onto Main Street, noting the signs for the Fried Festival—which elicited a snort and a smile—and followed the street to the town square. The place was exactly as he'd remembered it, as though it would forever be locked in a Normal Rockwell time warp. Other than new paint and a couple of new businesses he didn't recognize, the hub of Hydrangea was recognizably the same. He nodded to a couple of men who were busy setting up tables—in preparation for the festival, he imagined—and continued on. He made the circle, slowing as he passed the dance studio, before exiting via Daffodil Street to the back entrance.

Though savvy Realtors had come in and developed trendy studio apartments above many of the businesses around the square, his mother had done it out of necessity. She hadn't been able to afford both the business and a house, so she'd outfitted the studio first, then renovated the upstairs living quarters as money had permitted. The result had been an artist's den of sorts, with walls that didn't go all the way to the ceiling and lots of vintage treasures mined from yard sales and the Salvation Army. It had suited her, though, Bear thought now, but the place had always made him feel like a mismatched accessory.

He pulled up next to his mother's car and noted the open trunk with a sense of dread, then slid out from behind the wheel. Seconds later his mother dragged an enormous suitcase onto the balcony and waved impatiently at him.

"Finally," she said with a heavy dose of exasperation. "I was afraid I was going to miss you altogether."

Miss him? The dread bloomed into disbelief.

She started down the steps, awkwardly hauling the suitcase behind her. Impeccably dressed as always, she wore a blue linen pantsuit, ballet flats and a jaunty little beret. Pearl studs glowed from her ears and a small gold crucifix, the one she always wore, was nestled against her chest. "My flight leaves in three hours. It's international, which means I have to be there two hours early and it's a forty-five-minute drive. You know how I detest being late," she said, finally arriving at the bottom of the stairs. She stopped and looked up at him, then gestured to the bag. "Can you be a darling and pop this in the trunk for me?"

An international flight? She was leaving? Now?

He felt a disbelieving smile slide over his lips and gave himself a mental shake. This was his mother. Of course, she was leaving. So much for a new start, Bear thought as he stowed her bag and closed the lid.

"Where are you going?" he asked, his tone as conversational as if he was merely inquiring about the weather.

"To Paris," she said. "It's a retirement gift to myself." She glanced back at the house and studio. "I can't bear the idea of being around while you finish everything up. I've spent thirty-one years of my life here," she said. "I know this chapter is closing, but it's still tough, still going to take some getting used to."

And what better way to get used to it than by going to Paris? Bear thought. Especially when he'd be there to make sure that the repairs the new owner requested were done.

The brief brush with nostalgia complete, his mother released a resolute sigh. "The Salvation Army is coming to pick up the rest of the stuff left inside on Saturday afternoon," she said, "but if you find anything you think I might have put in by mistake, you can send it to my new address."

"You bought the house on Lilac Street?" She'd emailed a picture to him last month to see what he thought. The caption had read A Real Front Porch!

His mother pulled a piece of paper from her purse and handed it to him. "No," she said. "I bought a place in Charleston. A quaint little craftsman near the water."

He wouldn't give her the benefit of his surprise. "Charleston?"

She smiled at him as though she were merely sharing news with a passing acquaintance and not her son. "I'm going to sip mint juleps and join hoity-toity book clubs, go to estate sales and try my hand at painting. It's my turn," she said, as though her entire life hadn't been her turn. He could feel the old familiar irritation taking hold and redoubled his efforts to keep it in check. "I've left a list of the contracted repairs upstairs," she told him. "Please confer with Veda as you do them and make sure that everything is to her liking." She grimaced. "Naturally, I can't afford for the sale to fall through now."

And with the money she was saving on hiring a contractor, she could no doubt afford her trip to Paris. Sheesh. He was such a fool.

Veda? Why did that name sound familiar? He had a sudden memory of long golden hair and determined green eyes, skinned knees and a tattered tutu. Something in his chest gave a little squeeze and his heart inexplicably skipped a beat. Tiny Dancer? Tiny Dancer was the former student who had bought the studio? How old had she been when he left? Bear wondered. Twelve? Thirteen? She'd been young, he knew that. And so, so small. His nickname for her hadn't been the least bit original, but she'd gotten a kick out of it. He remembered his mother being exceptionally hard on Veda and when he'd asked her about it, she'd said she was only hard on the ones who had promise.

So what had happened to the promising young ballerina? Bear wondered. A husband and family most likely and, for whatever reason, the thought depressed him.

His mother glanced at her watch, then winced dramatically. "Goodness, I'd better get going. You have my cell phone number if you need me." She offered her cheek for a kiss, then smiled up at him. "We'll have a proper visit next time, yes? You would have been much too busy to be good company this time."

Yes, busy helping her. He gritted his teeth at his own stupidity. If there was a moron award, he would no doubt get it.

Rather than wait for his reply, she slid into her car and backed into the street, waving breezily as she pulled away.

A bark of dry laughter erupted from his throat before he could stop it.

And that, ladies and gentleman, was his mother.

2

VEDA HAYES HAD TOLD HERSELF that her recollections of Bear Midwinter's size were skewed from childhood memories, that he couldn't possibly be as large and intimidating as she remembered.

She'd been wrong.

From her vantage point in what would be her new home as soon as Bear finished the renovations, she could tell that he was not only bigger than she'd remembered, but he was also better-looking, as well.

Mercy.

There was simply…so much of him.

Bear was the wrong nickname, Veda thought as she watched him pick up his mother's giant suitcase and heave it into the trunk with utter ease. He was Atlas, she decided, imagining he was more than capable of holding up the earth. Those shoulders were a work of art within themselves. Combined with the imposing height, the perfectly proportioned, expertly muscled limbs and the sheer magnificence of his body, he was a walking, living, breathing Greek statue. From a strictly aesthetical viewpoint, she knew that he'd be beautiful naked.

Regrettably, that knowledge elicited a purely visceral reaction.

Cut high and tight in the traditional military manner, his hair was a burnished tawny gold and, were it not so short, she knew it would curl around his ears. High cheekbones carved intriguing hollows above the line of his angular jaw, creating the perfect palette for the dimples that appeared on each side of his mouth when he smiled.

He was smiling now, but even from this distance, she could see that he wasn't amused. It was an I-should-have-known grin, but had the same effect nonetheless. That smile did something funny to her insides, made them simultaneously tingle and melt. It was a familiar sensation where he was concerned.

There was something so innately thrilling about a man that large—that masculine—and it spoke to her on a purely base, physical level. It was a cavewoman gene she hadn't realized she'd possessed until she'd seen him again. She watched him scan the area around him, the careful way he held himself—not still, but steady—and, instinctively knew he'd cataloged every car in the lot, every entrance and exit on the back of the building, and had better familiarized himself with his immediate surroundings than she'd done after weeks of being back home. He was every inch the soldier, and that knowledge sent a little thrill through her.

As a young girl at On Your Toes dance studio, she'd been in utter awe of the teenaged son of her dance instructor. Bear had been smart and handsome and cool and most of the students had had a severe crush on him. Had you asked her twelve-year-old self, Veda would have found the word *crush* to be completely inadequate when it came to describing her feelings for Bear. She smiled, remembering. She would have insisted that she loved him, that they were soul mates, that he'd held her tender heart in the palm of his giant hand and that someday he was going to long for her as much as she'd pined for him.

Then he'd left for college and she'd been devastated.

Funny how one never fully got over a first heartbreak. The fissure might heal, but the pain of nostalgia was always waiting in the wings, ready to throb anew when the least little bit of memory was prodded. Just looking at him now, all these years and countless breakups later, she could feel the tightness in her chest, a flutter of nervous anticipation in her belly, the hot zing of attraction pumping through her veins.

From the moment her father had told her that Bear would be coming back to town to help his mother ready the place for sale, Veda had been locked in a state of nervous anticipation, a litany of what-might-have-beens playing in continuous circle through her head. It was ridiculous, really. She was an adult, ostensibly one who had a grasp on her emotions and yet that same familiar feeling of longing had risen up like Lazarus from the dead the instant she'd known she was going to see him again.

Madness, Veda thought.

But that was the trouble with Bear Midwinter—he'd always made her feel too much.

And considering she was trying to rebuild her life and start a new business, the last thing she needed to do was feel anything at all—other than gratitude that he was going to do the necessary repairs—for Bear. She sincerely hoped that self-preservation would kick in and keep her from doing something impulsively stupid.

Like drooling all over him.

Veda had always been very task-oriented, a list-maker, one of those organized people who got on everyone else's nerves. She did not find comfort in chaos and always operated with determination and a plan. She had her eyes on the prize. Set a goal, reach the goal, set a new goal. Her lips twisted.

It was that dogged perseverance that had completely derailed her latest five-year plan. Her mind had been so set on joining Jacque Bonnet's international dance team—what better way to see the world than dancing across it?—that she'd literally pushed herself past the breaking point. One too many stress fractures had put an end to what had been a very promising career. When she'd first realized that her days of performing were over, it had come as quite a blow.

Because she'd never considered the idea of failing, she'd never developed a backup plan. She'd never needed one. So it had seemed almost providential when her mother told her that Celeste had put her studio up for sale. With virtually no thought at all, which was totally out of character, she'd called her former dance instructor and made an offer.

While Veda had been packing up her place in New York and readying for the move back to Hydrangea, her father had inspected the studio and apartment, noted the repairs that needed to be done and handled the legwork necessary to facilitate the sale. She grinned. No doubt he would have jumped through hoops and a ring of fire to make sure that she came home.

This was, Veda was all too aware, the first step in her parents' latest goal, Operation Grandchild.

Her mother had never minded the dancing until she'd realized that (a) it was going to take her out of Hydrangea, (b) most of the eligible men in her field were gay and (c) lack of men meant less opportunity for marriage and having the grandchild her parents so desperately wanted to spoil.

She hadn't been back two days before her father had conveniently brought a "friend" home for dinner. Kurt was a twenty-eight-year-old accountant with more confidence than hair and soft, squishy hands.

Eww.

Next, her mother had insisted that Veda accompany her

to the courthouse to pay a parking ticket and had promptly steered her toward a group of Hydrangea's finest boys in blue. Kenny Watkins had been her mother's intended target and, while Kenny had certainly grown into a fairly attractive man, Veda wasn't interested. In grade school, she had once watched Kenny mine a giant booger from his nose and promptly eat it. She frowned.

That sort of thing stuck with a girl.

Currently, she was living in the carriage house at the back of her parents' property—virtually trapped and under constant surveillance—and simply could not wait to get moved in to her new home. She was used to having her own space and, while the carriage house was nice, the location was less than ideal. Were she to continue living there, she could imagine her parents' queuing men right up to her door.

Honestly, Veda wasn't averse to having a significant other—she was a bona fide romantic, appreciated the small gestures as much as the grand ones—and she'd certainly had her share of boyfriends over the years, though admittedly she couldn't confess to ever being in love. She'd been in like before, in fond, even. But love? That all-consuming can't-breathe-without-you sort of love?

Never.

Her gaze strayed to Bear, who was currently pulling his own bag out of the back of his rental car, and her chest gave an involuntary squeeze. No doubt the closest she'd ever come to real emotion, real love—though it had been the purely innocent variety—was what she felt for Bear Midwinter.

It was almost sad, really. And strangely...comforting.

How odd. She frowned, trying to pinpoint the source of the sentiment, then abandoned the effort as he made his way toward the stairs. He glanced at the window and his gaze caught hers. She inhaled, startled at the impact, then managed a breathless smile and gave an awkward little wave.

In the briefest of seconds, she watched recognition flash in those pale brown eyes—a golden amber that put her in mind of the tiger's-eye ring she'd worn on her right hand since her sixteenth birthday, which had been the reason she'd chosen it, of course—and then he smiled, really smiled, and her pathetic heart practically flipped in her chest, then thundered into a sprint that resonated in her ears so loudly, it left her nearly deaf. Her hands trembled and her body broke out in a prickly sweat that heralded impending nausea and her last thought, before she darted into the bathroom and emptied her stomach, was at least she wasn't puking on him…like she did the last time she'd seen him.

Thank God for small favors.

Only stage fright and Bear Midwinter had ever made her nervous enough to hurl. She'd eventually gotten over the stage fright.

Clearly, Bear was another matter.

3

BEAR WAS USED TO INSPIRING various reactions in women—usually an appreciative glance, an inviting smile, the occasional nervous giggle.

Causing one to vomit—twice now, for the love of all that was holy—was as novel as it was disturbing.

He watched Veda rinse her mouth in the bathroom sink and pat her flushed face before making her way back into the kitchen. His lips twisted. "It's official," he said with a matter-of-fact nod. "I make you sick."

Her watery green gaze shot to his and a startled laugh broke up in her throat. "No, I—"

He crossed his arms over his chest and leaned a hip against the counter, taking a covert inventory of the now fully grown Veda who stood before him. "There's no point in denying it," he said. "You tossed your cookies the last time I saw you, as well." He heaved a feigned, woebegone sigh. "Given the evidence—" he jerked his head toward the toilet "—I can only conclude that the mere sight of me makes you ill."

Meanwhile, the mere sight of her was making him anything but unwell.

She'd been a pretty little girl—big green eyes, sharp chin, a yard of silky blond hair. The woman she'd grown into wasn't so much pretty as striking. Those memorable green eyes—a startling shade that made him think of new moss on an old tree—set in that classically heart-shaped face was nothing short of arresting. Her skin was smooth and luminous, like moonlight on sand, and her nose was slim and straight. The mouth beneath it was a healthy pink, lush and unbelievably kissable.

An unexpected firebomb of attraction blasted through him, leaving him momentarily dumbstruck.

Bear Midwinter had never been rendered speechless. He wasn't sure what was more disconcerting—the instantaneous critical level of lust he'd just experienced or the sudden speech impediment.

Both, naturally, raised concern.

Hot for Veda? For Tiny Dancer?

It almost felt obscene. He'd known her since she was four, maybe five years old. For…twenty years. Jeez, had it been that long? It seemed impossible and yet the evidence stood before him, all five feet—he broodingly eyeballed her again—two inches of it. He'd missed the puberty years, obviously, because the last time he'd seen her, she hadn't had breasts or hips. But she did now, and the added dimension had given her a very womanly frame. Short and curvy, but fit all the same.

She blushed beneath his blatant stare and it belatedly occurred to him that he was being rude. He rubbed a hand over the back of his neck and shot her a sheepish smile. "You've changed a good bit since the last time I saw you."

She shrugged, her eyes twinkling. "One would hope. It's been twelve years. I threw up on you that time, so the way I see it, the toilet's an improvement."

"Are you saying it's going to be another dozen years before you stop vomiting altogether when you see me?" He tsked. "That's depressing. You're going to give me a complex."

She couldn't quite cover a snort. "I sincerely doubt it. And it's not you. It's just an unhappy, mortifying coincidence." Her eyes darted everywhere but at him. "I've felt off all morning. I guess my breakfast didn't agree with me."

He grinned. "That's one way of showing it who's boss."

She chuckled and shook her head. "I suppose."

He cast a glance around the loft, noting the empty walls and bare floors with an odd pang of regret. He supposed that was natural. While this had never been much of a home, it had been the only home he'd ever really known. Granted, he'd always felt more like an unwanted guest than a member of the family. Still, this was where he'd grown up, where he'd eaten cereal in front of the television, done his homework at the kitchen table, where he'd hidden his copies of *Playboy* underneath the floorboards, learned to shave and ultimately lost his virginity. He inwardly smiled, remembering. That had been one hell of a study date. He'd learned a lot.

He felt her gaze and from the corner of his eye, watched her bite her lip. "I guess this is a little weird for you, isn't it? Seeing it empty like this."

Bear sighed, wandering deeper into the living room. "It is," he admitted. He shot her a smile. "It's a lot roomier without Mom's stuff crammed in here."

She nodded toward a pile of things in the corner. "Celeste said you'd want to go through the things over there. She said they came out of your room."

He laughed darkly. "Then she must have packed it up a long time ago. She turned my room into her closet-slash-dressing room the week after I left for college. On the rare occasions I came home, I slept on the couch."

And he'd only done that when there wasn't an alternative. Thankfully, there'd been friends he could go home with most holidays and he'd worked during the summer, so that had kept him close to campus. He could count on one hand how many times he'd seen his mother during those college years and one of them had been at his graduation. She'd been late…and had left immediately following the ceremony. No card, no present, no congratulatory dinner. Good times.

What the hell was he doing here again?

"Well, she's left the bed in her room for you while you're working on things."

How thoughtful. And just what the hell was he supposed to do with it once he left? Ship it off to South Carolina? As if he would have time for that. Honestly, just when he thought she couldn't do anything more selfish—

"The Salvation Army is supposed pick it up when they come for the other stuff, but I was thinking about keeping it for the spare room. It's a lovely old iron bed."

It was. And it was unbelievably heavy. He had unpleasant memories of hauling it up the back staircase. He shot Veda a look. "What? You don't need a bigger closet and separate dressing room?"

She smiled. "Not at the moment." She cast another look around and released a small breath. "Right now I just need somewhere to live."

"Don't tell me you're homeless," he teased, intrigued by her especially grim tone. Intrigued by her, period. "Not in Hydrangea, land of sweet iced tea and hospitality."

She laughed again and shook her head. "Not homeless, no. I'm staying in the carriage house behind my parents' place until I can move in here."

He inclined his head, felt his lips twitch with humor. "And Mom and Dad are cramping your style, interfering with your game?"

She rolled her eyes. "Just the opposite, actually. I have no desire to play. And they keep putting Hydrangea's most eligible bachelors in my path." A droll smile caught the side of her ripe mouth and tugged. "Kind of hard to hide from them when I'm living in the backyard."

Ah, he thought, giving her a speculative glance. Now this was a very interesting turn of events. "Let me guess. You just came off a bad breakup and they're trying to get you back in the saddle."

Her eyes twinkled and she poked her tongue in her cheek. "Er, no."

He winced and kept fishing, far more curious than he should be. "Bad divorce then?"

She shook her head. "Sorry, wrong again. I've never been married."

Now, that was surprising. She was beautiful, smart and talented. He couldn't imagine that some good old boy hadn't at least tried to coax her down the aisle. Her choice then? And if so, why? Was she that particular? Or had something else gotten in the way? Other than the fact that she was buying his mother's place, he knew absolutely nothing about her, had no idea what she'd been doing during the last twelve years. Dammit, he was going to have to join Facebook, if for no other reason than to keep up with her.

"Ah," he drawled as understanding dawned. "So that's the problem then? They're afraid you're reaching your sell-by date?"

"In a manner of speaking, I guess," she said, chuckling at the analogy. "And they can hear the sound of my biological clock ticking much more loudly than I can." She gave her head a sad shake. "Evidently the grand-bird isn't enough anymore."

He blinked. "Grand-bird?"

"Odette, my African gray parrot. She's temperamental, but quite smart. She spent the first five years of her life in a nursing home and the next five in a barber shop. She's forever whining about her bunions and randomly quotes Jeff Foxworthy."

The bunion reference he could understand, but the other? "Jeff Foxworthy?"

She strolled to the window and glanced out over the square. "The shop owner was a fan. There are times I could cheerfully throttle him for that." She looked over at him and wry humor touched her gaze. "There are only so many you-might-be-a-redneck jokes a girl can take."

His eyes drifted over her again, lingering on the sleek curve of her hip. "I imagine so."

She hesitated, then blushed again. "I should probably get downstairs," she said. "My Twinkle Toes will be here in a few minutes. I only came up to get a few more measurements, see how much more furniture I'll need to buy to fill the place up. This loft is three times the size of my old apartment."

He arched a skeptical brow and glanced around. "You must have been living in a coat closet."

A grin rolled across her lips. "Close enough, but affordable square footage is hard to come by in New York."

Another surprise. "New York?"

She nodded. "I've only been back in town a couple of weeks."

"Experiencing culture shock?" he asked, wondering how his mother could have failed to mention that Veda had been living out of town. In New York, of all places. Of course, anything that didn't pertain directly to Celeste was of no consequence, so he really didn't know why he was surprised.

Veda grinned. "Not really," she said. "I miss the all-night coffee shop and Thai food, but otherwise, I've always been a Southern girl at heart. It's certainly different here, but ultimately Hydrangea is a good place."

He supposed. But he knew the town would be forever tainted by the memory of his miserable childhood and youth spent here. Certainly there'd been people he'd remembered who were kind, like Mrs. Johnston and Coach Crawford, but he hadn't gotten involved with many people in town. Even though his mother had never really wanted him around, she hadn't wanted him out and about, either. She always had something for him to do. While other guys had been out cruising the square or shooting pool at Moe's Burger and Tire, he'd been sanding floors, painting something or moving things around. His mother had loved to rearrange the furniture and he'd been the heavy lifter. He cast another glance about the room and felt the old familiar bitterness well up.

Not much had changed, really.

Which reminded him… "When you have a little time, I'd like to go over the list of repairs with you. You know, just to make sure that I know exactly what you want done."

"Sure," she said, looking strangely nervous. She tucked a stray strand of hair behind her ear. "I, uh…I'm teaching until six, but anytime after that would be fine." She brightened. "In fact, it would get me out of helping my mother perfect her supersecret entry into the fried-dessert cook-off, so that's definitely a win."

He laughed. "Supersecret entry?"

"Hey, the women in town take this cook-off seriously," she said, her eyes twinkling. "It's rumored that Reverend Morris is spying for his wife, paying visits to everyone who's rumored to enter. Mom won last year with her fried butter-pecan balls. She's got a title to protect."

"Such drama," he teased.

She nodded, chuckling softly under her breath. "It's entertaining, if nothing else."

He shrugged magnanimously. "Who needs theater?"

"Right." She backed toward the door. "See you at six then? Downstairs?"

"Sounds good. Do you mind if we discuss things over dinner?" he asked. He glanced toward the kitchen. "I'm sure my mother left nothing in the way of food here and—"

"Dinner's good," she said, shooting him a smile endearingly just short of shy. "The diner doesn't close until eight, so we're in business."

"Eight?" He'd forgotten that little detail about small-town living. They practically rolled up the streets after dark around here.

She winced. "That's been the biggest adjustment," she said. "If I want a latte after eight o'clock, the closest thing I'm going to find to it is in the machine at Chet's service center."

"What time does he close?"

"Ten…unless there's something he wants to watch on television. Then he's been known to close as early as six-thirty."

Bear snorted and rolled his eyes. "Good grief." A thought struck. "When does the hardware store close?"

"Five-thirty."

Right.

"But if you absolutely have to have something, Harris leaves the key under the flowerpot next to the front door. Just make sure you leave him a note of what you take so that he can put it on your account."

Bear felt a bemused smile drift over his lips and shook his head. He rocked back on his heels. "Only in Hydrangea."

She studied him for a second, the kind of probing regard that made him feel curiously exposed, transparent even, and irritatingly, he couldn't get a read on her expression. "It's got its perks," she said. And with that oddly enigmatic statement, she turned and left, leaving him alone for the first time in years in his former home.

Not surprisingly, he hated it.

4

A SUDDEN PRICKLING on the back of her neck and a tightness in her stomach told Veda faster than her eyes could confirm that Bear was watching her. Though she'd heard the door open and close many times over the last few minutes—common enough this close to the end of a class, when parents arrived to pick up their children—she nevertheless knew the exact instant when he came in. Had the atmosphere not instantly changed—she'd always been able to feel him—the sudden hush, followed by a spate of giggles, would have clued her in.

"Ms. Veda, there's a big man in here," Sophie Charles whispered loudly.

She felt her lips twitch and darted a glance across the room to where Bear stood. To her irrational annoyance, a cluster of women had already formed around him.

Tina Charles, Sophie's mother and a divorcée with big hair and surgically altered breasts, was currently eyeing Bear like the last éclair in the pastry case. Mandy Shipley, the bane of Veda's high school existence, who was also newly divorced and reputedly in search of her next victim, er, husband, had also joined the little group huddled around him. Mandy laughed loudly at something Bear said, then pressed her hand against his arm, as if he was just too funny for her to contain herself.

To her delight, Bear looked a little taken aback by Mandy's exaggerated laughter and smiled awkwardly down at her.

Knowing nothing would break up the flirting session faster than the patter of little feet, Veda quickly dismissed the girls and walked over to where Bear stood. "Just let me change and I'll be ready to go," she said with more than a little satisfaction. They didn't have to know that her dinner with Bear wasn't a date—they just needed to know that he was there for her. Petty? Shallow? Yes…and she rather liked it.

Both Mandy and Tina turned to look at her. "Showing Bear some of Hydrangea's Southern hospitality, are you, Veda?" Mandy asked, her smile a little sick and strained around the edges.

"Yes, but he's actually—"

Bear nodded and determinedly made his way to her side, then slung an arm around her shoulder and pressed a kiss to the side of her head. "She is," Bear said, effectively interrupting her, his voice low and disconcertingly intimate.

Had he not put his arm around her, she would have undoubtedly keeled over in shock.

He'd kissed her, Veda thought faintly. Sure it was just against the side of her head, but his lips had touched some part of her body and her body had reacted accordingly. A flash of heat boiled beneath her skin and concentrated in her breasts and areas farther south. Her pulse leaped in her veins, and a little thrill instantly arced through her.

"Veda and I go way back," Bear said, giving her another little squeeze. "We spent some time together in New York. I'm looking forward to catching up with her this week."

We spent some time together in New York? What the hell?

Mandy's gaze darted between the two of him—lingering over Bear's arm around Veda's shoulder specifically—then seemed to make herself smile. "Of course you are. We were certainly glad to hear that Veda was buying your mom's place. New York's loss was Hydrangea's gain."

"That's right," Tina chimed in, tightening her daughter's ponytail until the little girl winced. "It was really a shame that all those stress fractures ended your dance career, Veda, but at least you haven't had to abandon the field altogether. I'm sure you'll find teaching every bit as rewarding as performing."

She felt Bear's arm tense around her and knew it was in reaction to her own sudden anxiety. Funny how women had a way of saying cruel things under the guise of being polite. It was a mean-girl skill she never learned. "I'm sure I will," Veda told her, not certain of that at all.

Tina took her daughter's hand. "Come along, Sophie. Ms. Veda has plans—" she lingered over the word "—for this evening."

A chorus of goodbyes accompanied the rest of the group out the door. Veda locked up behind them, then collected herself and turned to face Bear. "What the—"

"Are they still hanging out on the sidewalk?" he asked, his tone grim and suspicious.

Veda casually peeked through the plate glass window as she flipped the sign to Closed. "Yes. Why did you—"

He peered around her. "Do they normally dawdle around like that?"

"It's not uncommon for the parents to spend a few minutes catching up before going their separate ways." She felt another blush burn her cheeks. "And you've certainly given them plenty to talk about. Why on earth did you lie to them?" She snorted. "'We spent time together in New York,'" she mimicked. "I haven't seen you in twelve years."

Honestly, she couldn't imagine what the hell he'd been thinking to imply that this was a date or that they were even as familiar with one another as he'd indicated. Yes, they were shameless flirts and he was admittedly a handsome new-comer, however brief his stay might be. And it had been un-believably gratifying to see the looks on their faces when he'd indicated that he preferred her company to theirs. Still…

Bear leaned a hip against the edge of her desk and gave her another one of those thorough once-overs that made her want to squirm. And maybe preen just a little.

"I lied to give us the history we're going to need to pull off the level of familiarity between us."

Level of familiarity? Wh—

He winced and rubbed the back of his neck. "I know I just threw you under the bus, but it was the quickest, most expedient way to put an end to a potential problem. I don't have the time or the inclination to get involved on any level with either one of those women and—" he chuckled, darkly "—believe me, I know the stalker-gleam when I see it."

She felt her lips twitch. "The stalker-gleam?"

"It's real," he insisted. "If I hadn't done something to deter them, I am confident that one or both would have turned up at Mom's apartment with some sort of casserole loaded with pro-cessed cheese, and a bottle of wine." He gave a little shudder.

She inclined her head knowingly. "Ah. And I'm the de-terrent then?"

He had enough grace to grin sheepishly. "You're an old friend helping out another old friend," he said. "And it could be to your benefit, too, you know," he said, quickly warm-ing to his topic. "If you play along, then you'll have an entire week without having to worry about who your parents are going to bring to your door."

She opened her mouth, a retort at the ready, then paused. Dammit, he had a point. A really good one, as a matter of fact. If her parents thought she was seeing Bear, they'd back off with the matchmaking attempts. No more surprise din-ner dates, no more pointless errands to arrange their own forced version of the meet-cute. "You sure know how to tempt a girl." She tapped a finger against her chin, still thinking. "And since I'll be moved out at the end of the week, it'll be harder for them to set me up with someone else."

"If you know that this is your last week in their guest house, then it's certainly occurred to them," he said, pressing his advantage. "They probably have someone waiting on you right now." He smiled, the wretch. "This is a win-win deal," he told her. "What do you think? Can you play along?"

Could she pretend to adore him? To hang on to his every word? Enjoy his company? Find him irresistible and fascinating? She released a small sigh.

Is this what they called life imitating art?

She'd always wanted to be Bear Midwinter's girl. Even if she was just the pretend variety, it was a whole helluva lot better than the nothing she would have ever been otherwise. So much for not doing something stupid. A mere kiss against her hair and she was putty in his hands.

Veda shrugged fatalistically. "Why not?" she said, expelling a long breath. "After all, you can't very well put my house in order if you're constantly fending off unwanted advances, can you?"

He smiled at her, those dimples she loved winking in his cheeks. "I knew you'd see it my way." He cocked his head and looked past her again. "They're still out there."

"They're curious," she said, shooting him a droll look. "Our so-called relationship is probably the most interesting thing to hit Hydrangea since the birth of Harold Meadow's five-legged goat."

He chuckled and his gaze skimmed over her face, lingering on her lips. "I bet that was a real spectacle."

Sweet heaven, if he didn't stop looking at her like that, she was going to be in serious danger of believing their make-believe relationship herself. If she didn't know any better, she'd think… Nah. Wishful thinking. She swallowed. "It was."

He strolled purposely forward and took her hand. Pressing a kiss against her fingers, he tugged her forward, more closely up against him. Her entire body tingled and she exhaled a breathless little gasp as he bent his head toward hers. "Then we should probably make sure we give them a good show, huh?"

His lips hovered just above hers, a mere hairsbreadth away, waiting for her consent.

Veda gulped. Her heartbeat thundering in her ears to a mash-up of "Hallelujah" and Etta James's "At Last", she smiled, then cupped the side of his face with her hand, skimmed her thumb along his woefully familiar cheek and uttered a barely audible, "P-probably so."

Less than a second later, Bear's beautifully sculpted lips met hers and the sensation that accompanied that initial touch was more explosive and thrilling than anything she'd ever experienced before. She felt him momentarily hesitate, as though he, too, was as startled by the connection, then he groaned low in his throat and deepened the kiss. It was deep and dark and sinful and he felt wonderful against her, so big and masculine, perfectly muscled, brilliantly proportioned.

His lips slid over hers with dizzying skill and his clever tongue tangled with and stroked hers, igniting a fire in her blood that made her hands tremble as they slid over his body. Her insides quaked with a feeling more rooted in primal need than generic desire.

His big hands framed her face, pushed into her hair, sending a prickling of gooseflesh over her scalp. He was gentle but sure, and the kiss was nothing short of bone-meltingly, thigh-tremblingly perfect. She breathed him in, inhaling the scent of his aftershave—something smooth and woodsy—

and he tasted like Butter Rum Life Savers, sweet iced tea and something else, something uniquely, singularly Bear.

In the dimmest recesses of her mind, Veda knew she was playing with fire. This was pretend, after all, and even if it wasn't, he would be leaving at the end of the week. A pitiful flicker of self-preservation lit her consciousness at the thought, but was quickly burned away by the heat licking through her veins. Her breasts felt heavy against her chest, her nipples beaded tightly behind her bra and a low, achy throb settled hotly between her legs. She barely resisted the urge to squirm against him.

Breathing heavily and with a reluctance that could only be described as flattering, Bear slowly ended the kiss. He rested his forehead against hers and smiled down at her. Humor and warmth and something else—surprise, maybe?—lit his twinkling, golden eyes. "Wow," he breathed. "You sure know how to…act."

Veda chuckled. "I just followed your lead," she said. A quick glance from the corner of her eye confirmed at least two people benefited from their performance. Tina Charles was green with envy and Mandy Shipley's mouth appeared to have unhinged from her jaw.

Sweet.

"Have you swallowed it already?"

She blinked. "What?"

"The canary," he said, chuckling. "That smile is more than a little self-satisfied." His gaze followed hers and his grin widened. "Ah, now I see."

She'd just bet he did. Oh, well. He wanted to pretend they were together to keep Mandy and Tina from stalking him. Was it her fault that an added benefit to that was making them jealous as hell?

"You've got your perks for our arrangement and I've got

mine," she said. "They're petty, I'll admit, but quite…gratifying."

He bent and kissed her again, just a brush of his lips against hers and another burst of sensation bolted through her. "Gratification is good."

Veda shuddered. It certainly was…and it came in so many different forms.

5

"Evening, Veda," the skinny waitress said, casting a speculative glance between the two of them. She nodded in his direction. "Evening, Bear. It's been a long time."

He frowned, trying to place the woman. He knew he should know her and yet...

"Nancy Jenkins," she said. "The last time I saw you, I was piling French fries on your plate at the high school. I always tried to give you a little extra. You might have been big, but you never quite looked like you had enough to eat."

Ah. He remembered her now. "Thanks, Nancy," he said, shooting a look at Veda across the table. If she thought anything was odd about Nancy's glib comment, she didn't betray it. While his mother had certainly never tried to starve him, keeping food in the house was never high on her list of priorities. It was mildly disconcerting to realize that people had noticed. "You're not at the high school anymore then?" he asked, for lack of anything better to say.

Nancy laughed and shook her head. "Goodness, no. I've gotten older and less tolerant. And kids have definitely gotten ruder." She nodded. "The diner suits me fine. If someone comes in that I don't like and I don't want to serve them, then me and Jenny—" she jerked her head in the direction of the other waitress on duty "—just switch out."

"What happens if neither one of you like the person who just came in?"

Nancy grinned. "We flip for it." She opened her order pad. "What can I get you to drink?"

Bear quirked a brow at Veda.

"I'll have a sweet tea," she said. He requested the same and, after a brief look at the menu, Nancy left with their order.

"She's quite a character," Veda remarked with a tilt of her head in Nancy's direction. "She'd left the high school by the time I'd come through."

Feeling a bit more relaxed, Bear leaned back against his seat and studied her thoughtfully. "Go ahead and make me feel old," he teased.

She snorted. "You're not old. You're what? Thirty-two?"

He would be. This week, as a matter of fact. "Not until Friday," he said, "so don't rush me."

She brightened, and for whatever reason, her pleasure made something in his chest shift. "Your birthday's Friday?"

Bear chuckled at her delighted expression. "Don't get so excited. It's just another day." One that his mother had never acknowledged, since that was the day he'd ruined her life. Hell, if it hadn't been for the other kids' mothers bringing cupcakes to school on their birthdays, he would have never known that it was supposed to be a big deal. Celeste had never made him a cake, much less given him a present.

"No, it's not," she admonished, scolding him playfully. "It's the only day of the year that's completely about you. It's your day."

He took a sip of the tea Nancy put in front of him and winced. "Whatever you say."

"I do say," she insisted. She leaned forward, her green

The Steadfast Hot Soldier

eyes sparkling with mischief. "What kind of fake girlfriend would I be if I didn't make sure your birthday was special?"

Fake girlfriend she may be, but she sure as hell kissed him like she meant it. His insides vibrated, just remembering. The first brush of her sweet lips against his had rocked him to the soles of his opportunistic feet, had made his ears ring, his skin prickle, his stomach flutter. It was hands down the very best kiss he'd ever had because he'd felt it…everywhere.

Had he been worried about those keen-eyed, eager divorcées at the studio? To a degree, yes. Call him old-fashioned, but when he was interested in a woman, he liked to pursue her, not vice versa, and that Mandy what's-her-name had all but posted a no-trespassing sign on his groin. And Tina hadn't been too far behind. Furthermore, he hadn't been lying when he said he didn't have time to avoid them, that pretending that he and Veda were an item would be beneficial and expedient.

That was all true.

And it was convenient, because the truth of the matter was…he'd just wanted to kiss her.

He'd taken one look at her this morning and felt as though he'd had the wind knocked out of him. It was more than mere attraction—attraction he understood and liked to think he could even control. But this… This was different. It was more potent, more thrilling, more substantial, for lack of a better description, than anything he'd ever experienced before. He looked at her and, the extreme sexual attraction aside, he felt something else…something new and elusive, almost haunting. It made him ache and, irrationally, he knew she was the only person who could make it stop.

Nancy slid their meals in front of them, and Veda noticed the especially large servings on his plate with a wry arch of her brow.

"Don't get your feelings hurt, sweetie," Nancy told her. "Given those delicate bones of yours, you need to be careful about how much weight you put on them." She patted Veda on the shoulder and quickly moved on to check her other tables.

Looking adorably mortified, Veda glanced heavenward and chewed the inside of her cheek. "Why did I move back here again?"

Bear grinned and forked up a bite of meat loaf. "Don't ask me. You're the one who was telling me that it had perks."

"It does," she said grimly. "I'm just having a hard time remembering what they are at the moment. Honestly…"

"So, based on Tina's comment and now Nancy's, I'm assuming that these stress fractures of yours had something to do with your sudden change in career and subsequent move back to town?"

She avoided his gaze and skewered a few green beans. "That's a fair assumption."

Damn. Given the amount of dedication and discipline required for that kind of career, he couldn't begin to imagine what she was feeling. But he knew that disappointed was barely the tip of the iceberg. He frowned. "I'm sorry, Veda."

She looked up at him then and a sad smile shaped her lips. "I am, too," she said, heaving a small sigh. "But life goes on. Not in the way I'd originally, painstakingly planned it, but in a new direction." She swallowed. "I won't lie and say that I wasn't initially devastated, because I was." A tiny frown marred her brow. "Heartbroken, too, because I'd dedicated so much of my life to the ballet. But then I heard about your mom selling the studio and, though I'd never had any desire to teach, I suddenly wanted it. Needed it." She shrugged. "And here I am."

"For what it's worth, I think you'll make a wonderful teacher." He grimaced. "Certainly a nicer one than my mother ever was."

Veda chuckled. "Your mother was an excellent teacher.

Strict, yes. Critical, definitely, and occasionally quite mean. But still very good."

"That's just a polite way of saying she was an autocratic maniacal bitch."

Her eyes widened and she choked on her drink. "Bear."

"You're just too nice to say it," he told her, peering at her above his fork. "Tell me I'm wrong."

"You're wrong," she said, eyes twinkling. "You left out selfish."

"Ah, how could I have left out selfish?" he asked, laughing softly. He, more than anyone else, knew just how selfish she was.

She sobered a bit, seemed to be looking at something he couldn't see. "But she was still a good teacher. I wouldn't have had the skill to make it as far as I did without her and I'll always be grateful to her for that."

Well, if that ended up being his mother's only good deed—however inadvertently—at least it had been to Veda's benefit. That was something at least.

"Do you really think you're going to like it here?"

Instead of patronizing him with a quick yes, she considered his answer for a minute. "Yes, I do," she finally told him. "It's going to require some adjustment, but Hydrangea is home, after all. And I do love the girls."

"But..." he prodded.

She smiled at him and looked away. "What makes you think there's a but?"

He waited, shot her a knowing look.

She sighed and her gaze tangled with his once more. "But...I will miss performing."

"Of course, you will," he said, as though it were a foregone conclusion.

She winced. "You don't think that makes me vain?"

Bear felt his eyes widen. "Why the hell would it make you vain? You trained to perform. Performing was the goal."

She stilled for a moment, and a slow-dawning smile broke across her lips. "You're right," she said, as though he'd just answered one of the many questions of the universe. "I'd never thought of it that way."

He grunted, unreasonably pleased. "You should have asked a man. Men are typically more logical than women."

She gasped, then wadded her napkin and threw it at him. "Smart-ass."

"Careful," he warned. "I'm the smart-ass who's completing the repairs on your new home and studio."

Her smile dimmed a little and became more sympathetic. "I'm really sorry about that," she said. "Had I known she was going to rope you into renovating for free, I would have asked for a local contractor."

"What?" he teased. "And miss the chance to be your pretend boyfriend?" He shrugged. "Don't worry about it."

"You didn't know she was going to Paris, did you?"

He glanced up at her. "What gave it away? My slack-jawed expression when I saw her haul her luggage down the stairs?"

Her expression darkened. "That was shitty."

He grinned without humor. "That's my mother. My expectations aren't very high."

"Nevertheless, it's not like you come home—or can come home—that often. She shouldn't have asked you to do the work for her and she damned sure shouldn't have left it with you the way she did." Veda scowled. "I'm sure you could have spent the time doing something you actually wanted to do." She glanced at him again, still adorably outraged on his behalf. "I'm truly grateful, Bear, even if she's not, and I am more than willing to help in any way I can. I've got classes during the day, but my evenings are free."

Strictly speaking, he didn't really need the help, but the company would be nice.

Especially hers.

He nodded. "I'd appreciate it, thanks."

He let his gaze drift over her face once more, noting the sleek slope of her pale brows, the especially curly lashes framing her pretty green eyes, the plump ripeness of her bottom lip, and felt his groin tighten, his palms itch with the need to feel her skin beneath his hand.

She blushed beneath his stare, a rosy-pink that made her skin glow, and fidgeted with a ring she wore on her right hand. She looked away and cleared her throat. "Speaking of the repairs," she said. "Thankfully, your mother took better care of the studio than she did the loft, so the work that needs to be done downstairs can wait until the end of the week. If it's all right with you, I'll probably go ahead and start moving some furniture and things in as you finish."

"Of course," he said. His mother might have left him a bed, but not much else. There wasn't so much as a chair in the apartment. As a matter of fact, if Veda wanted him to take things a room at a time so that she could actually go ahead and start moving in a little every day, he was fine with that. "I'll focus on one room at a time during the day and we can move your stuff in at night."

She hummed under her breath, considering the suggestion, and then smiled. "If you're sure it's not going to get in your way, I'd love to do that. And I really don't have all that much, so…"

"Why don't I start with the kitchen and living room?" he suggested. "I'll paint both those rooms first thing in the morning, then fix the leak under the sink and take the doors off the kitchen cabinets like you asked." He quirked a brow. "Do you want to keep those?"

"I'd better," she said after a moment's pause. "I don't anticipate going anywhere anytime soon, but if I ever sell the place, the new owners will probably want them. It's an idiosyncrasy of mine. I just like being able to see exactly what I have. It also forces me to be neat, which is a good thing."

He'd noticed that when he'd gone into the studio. His mother's desk had always been cluttered with papers, various hairpins and ribbons. Veda's had been tidy, everything stowed in little mesh trays, a vase of calla lilies on the side.

"Have you picked out all of your paint?"

She nodded once. "I have. Harris has everything waiting for me at the hardware store."

The bell over the door chimed, signaling a new customer. Or in this case, customers—Tina and Mandy walked in and took the booth directly across the aisle from them. They both smiled at him and barely glanced in Veda's direction. For reasons that escaped him, their blatant disregard of her infuriated him to no end. It made him want to haul her across the table and kiss the hell out of her again, if for no other reason than to prove to them that she mattered, that he preferred Veda's company to theirs.

From the corner of his eye he saw both waitresses in a hushed argument. Then Nancy pulled out a coin and tossed it into the air. He chuckled under his breath and signaled Veda to look with a significant jerk of his head. She did and then laughed softly.

Her eyes twinkled. "Can't say that I blame them for that."

He couldn't, either. It was Nancy who lost the toss and reluctantly made her way toward the table. Bear quirked a brow. "You about ready?"

At her nod, he dropped enough cash to cover the bill—and a sizable tip for Nancy in thanks for all those extra helpings over the years—onto the table, then slid out of the booth and offered Veda his hand. Hers felt so small in his, so delicate, and another wave of possessiveness washed through him.

"Have I ever mentioned that you're gorgeous?" he asked her, low enough to sound intimate, but loud enough to make sure that their audience heard him. "Because you are, you know."

Veda started a bit at the unexpected compliment. She momentarily froze, darted a look at the women behind him, then found his gaze again and a knowing smile just shy of smug bloomed over her lips. "You might have mentioned it before, but it's one of those things a girl never gets tired of hearing, so thank you."

He threaded his fingers through hers and gave a squeeze. "You're welcome." Whistling tunelessly, he followed her out the door, then drew her to him and dropped another kiss on her lips. "Just so we're clear, that wasn't just for their benefit," he said. "I meant it."

And he did.

6

"VEDA GRACE, OPEN THE DOOR. It's your mother."

As if anyone else ever called her Veda Grace. Or would
have had the nerve to knock on her door at—she cast a bleary
eye at the clock on the microwave as she shuffled through
the kitchen—six-thirty in the morning.

She groaned.

Odette fluffed her feathers behind her drape and squawked
in protest at the disturbance. "My feet are killing me," she
said in her high-pitched voice. "It's hell gettin' old."

With an impending sense of doom and another mental
hack at the imaginary umbilical cord her mother couldn't
seem to sever, Veda braced herself for an onslaught of questions and unlocked the door. Her mother blinked her perfectly
mascara'd lashes at her daughter's unkempt state and tsked
lamentably. "Goodness, dear, you'd frighten the warts off a
toad with that hair. You really need to take the time to brush
it out before you go to bed."

Perfectly put together as always—expertly styled hair,
flawless makeup, iron creases along her sleeves and pants—
her mother followed her into the house. Much to her mother's
chagrin, Veda hadn't inherited her attention to detail when
it came to her personal appearance. No, she wasn't one of

those people who wore pajamas to the grocery store, but still, she didn't consider makeup a prerequisite for leaving the house, either.

"I shower in the mornings," Veda said, turning around and backtracking into the kitchen. She could tell that this talk was going to require caffeine.

"Your father and I held dinner for you last night, but you never came home," she said lightly, about as subtle as a sledge-hammer, as usual.

Veda filled the kettle with water and set it on the stove. "Mom, I've told y'all not to do that. I am perfectly capable of feeding myself." Hell, it's not as if she was a giant baby bird, waiting in the nest with her mouth open. She was an adult who was perfectly capable of making her own food, or buying it prepared, if need be.

"We enjoy sharing meals with you," her mother said. "A call would have been appreciated. I'd invited that nice Kenny Watkins over for dinner. It was quite awkward when you didn't show up."

Veda pulled a couple of mugs down from the shelf and popped a tea bag into each one. She waited on her eye to stop twitching before she turned to glare at her mother. "It wasn't awkward for me," she said. "Because I'm not the one who invited him."

Her mother scowled and looked away. "Imagine my surprise then this morning, when I ran into Nancy Jenkins on my walk and she tells me that you were at the diner with Bear Midwinter. She said she'd heard you and Bear had seen each other while you were in New York and that y'all appeared to be 'rekindling your romance' while he was in town." She looked expectantly at Veda, her brows climbing her forehead. "I'd had no idea that you'd ever had a romance at all, much less one that you were interested in rekindling."

Guilt pricked at her conscience, taking a bit of the wind

out of her self-righteous sails. Her mother, in her own misguided, unwanted way, was trying to help her. Bear's mother hadn't seen him in years and instead of using his leave as an opportunity to spend some time with her son, she'd left him to go to Paris. She really needed to be more appreciative, Veda thought.

She handed her mother a cup of tea. "It was brief," she said, hating to lie, but left with little choice at this point. She knew the gossip vine in Hydrangea was well and thriving, but she'd expected to have a little more time.

"But you never said a word," she said. She rolled her eyes and snorted indelicately. "And given the crush you had on that boy, I would have thought that anything with Bear would have been something you'd have shared, brief or not."

Veda felt her cheeks burn. "You knew?"

Her mother smiled knowingly. "The various Veda loves Bear, VH and BM and Veda Midwinter scribbles all over your notebooks gave you away," she said, hiding a little grin behind her teacup. "He was always a nice boy. Smart, thoughtful, responsible." She tsked. "A credit to his mother, though her raising couldn't have been what produced that character. I know that you cared for her, Veda, but she was truly a horrible woman." She frowned. "I've never met a more selfish person in my life."

It was true that Veda had loved Celeste when she'd been a girl. And, as she'd told Bear, she knew that she wouldn't have made it as far as she had along her original career path had it not been for his mother. But watching her yesterday—seeing her blatant disregard for her son—had triggered a dislike and disgust for her former instructor the likes of which she'd never known, and an ache for Bear that made her heart hurt.

He deserved so much better.

"So it's true then?" her mother asked. "You're seeing him?"

Veda nodded. In for a penny, in for a pound. And though

she knew it wasn't real, it was still a dream come true. How could she pass up this opportunity? Especially when he looked at her the way he had last night, as though he really did think she was gorgeous, as if he really wanted to kiss her.

Her mother's expression remained neutral, but a flash of something—disappointment, maybe?—momentarily lit her gaze and she took another sip of her tea.

Veda didn't know what sort of reaction she'd expected, but this certainly wasn't it. "I thought you'd be pleased," she said. "You've been parading every single Tom, Dick and Harry in front of me since I got here."

"I do want you to date," she said.

Ah... It was who she was dating that her mother didn't approve of. Irritation spiked and she felt her eyes widen. "I thought you liked Bear. Only a moment ago you were talking about how wonderful he was." She didn't understand it. "How can you not like Bear?"

Her mother heaved a sigh. "Oh, do calm down, Veda. It's not that I don't like Bear—I do. I think he's a very fine young man with lots of admirable qualities."

"But...?" she prompted.

Her mother smiled sadly, her eyes soft with concern. "But he's a soldier, Veda. A Ranger. Career military. And he's only here for the week. My concern is what's going to happen at the end of it."

"Mom, I—"

Her mother silenced her with a look. "I know how you felt about that boy, Veda. I know that you were heartbroken when he left. I watched you pine for him for years after that departure." She glanced meaningfully at the ring on her finger and arched a knowing brow. "I understand that you eventually dated other guys and have had the odd boyfriend or two, but you've never let it get serious. The moment someone started to care too much, you ended the relationship. You'll argue that you're an adult with adult feelings and that you know what you're doing and nobody hopes more than I do that you're right. But I think you need to consider the consequences if you're wrong." She paused, her gaze turning inward as she looked at something Veda couldn't see. "Every girl has a first love story, a first crush. But Bear Midwinter was more than that to you." Her gaze found Veda's once more. "It was real for you. And if it was real then, I can only imagine what it will be to you now." Her mother reached across the bar and smoothed the hair away from Veda's face, a familiar gesture. "Please tread carefully."

Stunned at her mother's insight—she'd understood much more than Veda had ever given her credit for—she released a shaky breath and lied again.

"I will."

Odette squawked again. "If you've ever woken up with a black eye and a hickey…you might be a redneck."

Never more thankful for one of Odette's ill-timed Jeff Fox-worthy impressions, Veda giggled.

Her mother rolled her eyes, then gathered her purse and headed for the door. "That bird needs to learn some new jokes."

"It could have been worse," Veda told her. "That barber could have been an Eddie Murphy fan."

Her mother stopped short, her hand on the knob, and gave a little shudder. "Heaven forbid. Dinner will be ready at a quarter after six," she said briskly. "I'll set a place for Bear."

"What? I—" The door shut on her protest.

Oh, hell.

EMMALINE HAYES walked through her kitchen directly into her husband's arms, choking back a sob as tears burned the backs of her lids. "Oh, Redmond, we're too late. It's all true. I'd hoped, but— She's seeing him."

She felt him sigh, his big chest deflating under her cheek as he stroked her back. "Maybe it won't be as bad as you think," he said. "She's older now. She's not a young impressionable girl."

Emmaline drew back and swept a tear from beneath her eye. "No, she's not. She's an adult who has never quite gotten over him. And now he's here and interested in her. You saw the look on her face when we told her Bear was coming back, that he'd be the one working on the place." She swallowed hard, then stepped away from him. Taking a deep breath, she pulled the latest batch of batter for the fried contest out of the fridge, then turned the heat on beneath the oil. "He'll just leave again, and then what will happen to our girl? I want her to settle down, to have a home and family, to love someone who loves her back, to have what we have." She shrugged into her apron and tied it around her waist. "I thought when she moved back home that the natural order of things would take their course, but—"

"Emmaline, you don't know that they're not."

"And then Celeste just had to insist that Bear be the one to do the repairs, even though I told her I would see to them myself, even pay for them." She growled low in her throat. "That woman is just evil. She could have still gone to Paris and let her son actually go on a vacation or something while he was on leave, but no. She wanted him to do them. She said that he owed her that much." She snorted. "No one owes Celeste Midwinter a damned thing, least of all her poor son. The only person that woman has ever cared for is herself."

"I didn't know that you'd told Celeste you'd hire a contractor and pay for the repairs yourself," her husband remarked in a too-casual tone.

Whoops. "Trust me, Redmond, it would have been worth it to save our daughter from seeing him again. This was supposed to be a new start for her. But now she's starting it off with him…" Emmaline tested the oil and shook her head. "It's a recipe for heartache. You know it as well as I do." She squeezed her eyes shut and swore under her breath. "If only we could have got her interested in someone else before he got here."

"We tried, Em," Redmond told her. "And I'm not convinced that was going to work anyway. Veda has always had a mind of her own."

Maybe so, but Emmaline knew her daughter had given her heart away at twelve, possibly sooner, and had never quite gotten it back. She ought to know—she'd done the same thing herself. She'd recognized her daughter's unusual heartbreak for what it was when it had happened because she'd been through it first. She had firsthand experience of the depth of feeling, the agony. She cast a glance at Redmond and felt her heart give an involuntarily little jump, still felt that indescribable thrill bubble through her when she looked at him.

Redmond Hayes had been six years older than her. He'd lived next door and she'd known the first time she'd ever laid eyes on him that she was going to marry him someday. She'd followed him around like a little lost puppy dog, looked for or made up reasons to "drop by" his house and equally hated and envied the girls he'd dated.

She'd spent more time in the tree in their backyard that looked into his bedroom window than she had in their house the summer she'd turned thirteen. It had been his last summer at home before leaving for college at Ole Miss and she'd watched him pack up with a lump in her throat the size of Texas and an empty ache in her heart that plagued her until he graduated and moved back to Hydrangea.

Only he hadn't come alone. He'd brought a fiancée with him.

Luckily for Emmaline, the fiancée was two years younger

and hadn't finished her degree yet. Her parents were adamant that the two not marry until she'd finished school.

Because giving up had never occurred to her, Emmaline applied for a job as a part-time secretary at Redmond's newly opened accounting firm and badgered him into hiring her. She'd been seventeen, fully developed and still hopelessly in love with him. She'd never put a toe over an inappropriate line, but rather took advantage of those hours to truly get to know him and let him get to know her. Despite the age difference—and admittedly, there was still quite a gap between a seventeen and twenty-three year old—they'd become fast friends. The bond she'd always known was there strengthened and, though it took longer for him to see past the age difference and really see her, he finally did midway through her senior year. It was just glance, a lingering puzzled look, but she'd recognized it all the same.

Pressing her advantage, she only put through half the calls from his fiancée and made her dates pick her up at his office. Ruthless? Yes. But so worth it. By the time her prom had rolled around, he'd broken off the engagement and had started casually finding fault with every guy she went out with. If he knew she had a date, he'd invent reasons for her to work late to prevent her from going. She inwardly smiled, remembering. Oftentimes she'd lie and tell him she had a date simply to spend more time with him.

The night she'd graduated from high school, he'd asked her to stay on at the firm. He'd offered her a raise and the flexible hours she'd need to complete her nursing degree—though she'd ultimately gone into business management instead—and then he'd asked her out. He'd been endearingly nervous, more so than she'd ever seen him, and worried about what her parents would think.

"Listen, Emmaline, are you sure? Your dad is going to want my head on a platter."

"My dad will get over it."

He had, much more easily than anyone had anticipated. A month later they'd married.

Though she wished she could see the same kind of outcome for Veda, Emmaline knew there were huge obstacles in place and her biggest enemy was time.

Redmond had returned to Hydrangea because his family had been here, had ties to the community.

Bear, she knew, didn't. The military had become his home and, even if he ultimately cared enough about Veda to want spend the rest of his life with her, Emmaline feared it would be Veda who'd be the one to relocate, not the other way around. She'd lose her little girl all over again.

But if that's what it took to make her daughter happy, then so be it. Emmaline would do all she could to help. Unfortunately, Veda only had a week to bring Bear around. She hoped that was enough.

7

BEAR WAS WAITING when Harris Brown arrived to open the hardware store. Dressed in a navy blue T-shirt and a pair of work jeans, the proprietor was exactly as Bear had remembered, only a little more lined and gray. He smiled in welcome and offered the traditional nod. "Mornin', Bear. Ready to get started, I see."

"Morning," Bear returned. The smell of paint, lawnmower oil and lemon cleaner hung in the air and the old wooden floorboards creaked beneath his shoes as he followed the older man inside. "And yes, sir, I am."

Harris flipped on lights as he moved through the building, then rounded the counter and turned on the computer and coffeepot. "I'll need to get my drawer out of the back," he said, jerking a finger toward his office. "I've got Veda's paint all ready to mix."

Bear pulled a list from his front pocket and handed it to the older man. "I'm going to need this stuff, as well."

Harris's wirelike brows drew together and his lips moved as he silently reviewed the items. "I've got all of this in stock," he told him. He looked up. "You're thorough and you mean to do a proper job of it. I like that," Harris remarked with a nod of approval.

For whatever reason, the older man's regard settled warmly around Bear's middle.

"Too many people don't value doing a job right anymore. They want the quickest, easiest, cheapest fix. Only by the time they've repaired something a couple of times—same amount of time, same amount of labor, same amount of money—they might as well have done it the right way to start with. I tell 'em that, but they ignore me." He sighed, looked over the list again. "Right. It'll take me about fifteen minutes to get this all pulled together. You're welcome to stay here and wait, but Ms. Ella's just opened the dry goods store and I know she's anxious to see you. She's usually got some muffins and what-not there in the morning."

Bear nodded. He'd been looking forward to seeing Ms. Ella, as well. She'd always been unbelievably kind to him. She'd made a point to come to his football games in high school and had never failed to get him a little something for his birthday. She was sort of like the grandmother he'd never had. Truth be told, he'd kept in touch more with her over the years than he had his mother, probably because Ella actually liked to hear from him. "Then I'll head on over there now."

Harris grinned. "Brace yourself for a scolding. She expected you yesterday."

Laughing softly under his breath, Bear shook his head and moved toward the door. The bright glow of early-morning light filtered through the live oaks, sugar maples and magnolia trees that stood sentinel around the square, casting dappled shadows on the sidewalk under his feet. The sweet scent of hydrangeas perfumed the air and the little town was just coming to life, preparing for another day. A few people strolled along the sidewalks, mostly seniors getting their exercise, and an occasional car rounded the square. The barber shop door was already propped open and a few workers had resumed preparations for the Fried Festival. More tables and

banners—Get Your Grease On!—had gone up since yesterday when he'd arrived.

An odd pang of nostalgia struck him as he surveyed the
scene, one that he didn't understand and couldn't explain, but
couldn't deny all the same. What would his life have been
like had he stayed here? Bear wondered. What would he have
done? What career path would he have chosen? He'd never
considered those questions before, but he couldn't shake the
sensation that he might have missed out on something important. It made him wonder what he'd do now, if he suddenly decided that the military was no longer for him. It was
madness and yet...

"Bear Midwinter, as I live and breathe!"

Ella Johnston, her face wreathed in a smile of delight, set
her broom aside and opened her arms wide.

Bear grinned, then strolled forward and hugged the older
woman. She smelled like lotion, fabric softener and sugar
cookies. Familiar. "Ms. Ella," he said.

She drew back so that she could properly see him better.
"Goodness, let me get a look at you," she said, her faded blue
gaze as sharp as ever, roaming over him. "A sight for sore
eyes, I tell you," she said, nodding approvingly. "Looks like
you're eating well. Still enjoying the military?" she asked.
"I wouldn't know because I haven't heard from you in more
than a year," she scolded, shooting him a pointed look over
her shoulder as she made her way into the store. "Not even
a Christmas card."

His conscience twinged. "I'm sorry. I was in Afghanistan
until a couple of months ago."

She hummed under her breath and nodded knowingly.
"No doubt doing top secret things that you aren't permitted
to tell me about."

He merely grinned. As if he would tell her anyway. War
was hell and the little village he'd been in was so far removed

from Hydrangea, he wouldn't have been able to describe it adequately anyhow. Truth be told, he was sick of war, the death and destruction, the constant moving, the lack of a proper home with a proper bed. But he didn't know anything else and, ultimately…he had nowhere else to go.

Home, at least in the sense of being around family, had never been an option.

Ella handed him a cup of coffee and a muffin. "So I hear your mother is moving to Charleston," she said.

Bear nodded, his gaze scanning the familiar store. The technology, to his odd relief, seemed to be the only thing that had been updated. The same glass countertops and display shelves were in place, as was the old pinball machine against the back wall. He inwardly grinned. He'd dropped many a quarter into that machine. "It would seem so."

"And she's not coming back here at all? After her vacation is over, she's going directly to her new home?"

"As far as I know," Bear told her.

Ella's mouth tightened. She'd never been a fan of his mother. "Well, I'm sure glad that you're here. Gives me a chance to see you," she said, smiling up at him, a halo of snowy curls around her face. She might have grown older, but she was just as spry as he remembered. Ella had always had a secret spark of some sort, one that had never failed to draw him in.

"How have you been?" he asked. He darted a meaningful look outside. "Are you ready for the Fried Festival?"

Her blue eyes twinkled with humor and she nodded mysteriously. "I'm ready," she said. "This year I'm going to give Emmaline Hayes a run for her money in the dessert category. I've been perfecting my recipe for months."

"Seriously?"

"You bet," she said. "I'll admit her butter pecan balls were better than my chocolate dreams, but last year I wasn't really trying. This year I'm bringing my A game." She paused and shot him a curious look. "You're not here spying for her, are you?"

Bear felt his eyes widen. "What?"

"Word is that you're seeing Veda," she said, giving him a speculative look. "It's not too much of a leap."

"Yes, it is," he told her with a disbelieving laugh. Jeez, Lord. Veda hadn't been kidding when she said the townspeople took these competitions seriously. "I'm not spying for anybody. I just came down here to see you while Harris is getting my supplies together."

"Well, good," she said, seemingly mollified. "And it's good that you're seeing Veda, too. She's a sweet girl. We were all glad to hear that she was taking over your mom's place."

Honestly, from what he'd been able to discern, there wasn't a single person who was sad to see his mother go. How was that possible? How had she lived in this town for so long and not managed to have a single friend?

Ella hesitated. "Your mother was a good dance instructor, Bear, but—" She paused, seemingly looking for a diplomatic way to finish the sentence. "She was never what one would call...neighborly."

Narcissists typically weren't, Bear thought with a wry grin. "I understand."

"You couldn't be less like her. You were always such a friendly boy. Courteous, respectful, kind." She smiled warmly at him. "In your case, the apple might have fallen from the tree, but somehow ended up in another orchard altogether."

Bear chuckled. "Thank you."

"You're welcome," she said, nodding once more. "Don't be a stranger this week, or after you leave again, either. You're Hydrangea's son, whether you or your mother lives here or not. We're proud of you."

Touched and strangely shaken, Bear smiled. "I appreciate that, Ella."

"Do you need anything?" she asked, gesturing around the store. "I noticed that the mover's loaded up your mother's things. I'm hoping she left enough there for you to be comfortable while you do that work for her."

That would have been nice, but not true to her character. He winced. "Actually, I need to get a couple of towels and washclothes."

He'd brought his own toiletries, of course, but hadn't realized until he went to shower that she hadn't left him anything to dry off with. He'd had to use the sheet from the bed and it had been damned awkward.

Ella scowled, presumably at his mother's thoughtlessness. "Right," she said. "Tell you what. I'm going to put a care package together for you and send it over with Mark, my delivery boy, this afternoon."

"Ella, you don't have to—"

"I know I don't have to," she said. "I want to. And if you think of anything at all that you need, then you just call me and let me know."

It was odd having someone fuss over him, Bear thought. Odd, but nice. "I will, thanks."

She peered around him and smiled. "Ah, Harris is waving, dear," she said. "He must have your supplies together. I'll have soup and sandwiches at the counter today for lunch. I know you're going to be busy, but you need to take time to eat and if your mother failed to leave you a towel—" her voice darkned ominously "—then I doubt she thought of food, either. Oh, and before I forget—" she reached into her pocket and pulled out a small white bag "—these are for you."

He knew before he looked into the little bag what he'd find—chocolate stars.

Bear hugged her again and pressed a kiss against her lined cheek. "Thanks, Ella."

"You're welcome, Bear. It's good to have you home."

Home? The word startled him, but for lack of a better description, he supposed that's what Hydrangea was for him. And Veda had been right. Given the kindness he'd been shown since he got back into town yesterday, the little place did have its perks.

And she, of course, was one of them.

Honestly, if anyone had told him that he'd be all tied up in knots over Veda Hayes—Tiny Dancer, of all people—Bear would have never believed it. Until yesterday, on the rare occasions he'd thought about her, she'd remained as he'd remembered her—a young girl with eyes too big for her face and a penchant for blushing every time he looked at her. Refreshingly, she still blushed, but she'd grown into those eyes, right along with the rest of her. She was lovely, with a wry self-deprecating sense of humor and a mischievous streak that was downright sexy.

Physical attraction aside—and admittedly that attraction was fierce—there was more to Veda, an indefinable something that made him want to get to know her better, to be around her. She excited him. He'd barely slept for thinking about it, thinking about her and that kiss, the way her lips had fit just so over his, the feel of her small, supple body against his own. He hardened, just thinking about it. She was petite and sweetly curved, but there was a strength there, as well, one that he admired and appreciated.

She was different, Bear decided, unlike any woman he'd ever met before and, though they were only supposed to be pretending to date, he could already tell the line was getting blurred.

And the hell of it? He didn't care.

8

SHE'D KNOWN DINNER WITH HER parents had been a bad idea, Veda thought later that evening. Her face so flushed she felt like it was on fire, she opened the door to the carriage house and resisted the urge to curl up in a ball and die from mortification. "I am so sorry about that," she said, still unable to face Bear.

It hadn't been a friendly get-to-know-you dinner—more like the damned Spanish Inquisition. Her mother had been horrible. She'd asked Bear more personal questions about his life and his plans than she imagined the immigration bureau required.

He chuckled under his breath. "No worries," he said with a deep exhale. "Though, I admit I was a little alarmed over the hooker comment. I didn't realize that everyone assumed that all men in uniform were frequent visitors to houses of ill repute." He snickered, his voice cracking with humor.

She hung her head. "I am so sorry."

Honestly, she didn't know what the hell was wrong with her mother or what she'd been trying to prove with that incessant line of questioning about career and his future plans. Actually, she did know, and it humiliated her all the more. Her mother was trying to prove her point, that a future with Bear in Hydrangea was about as likely as another five-legged goat.

She knew there was no future with Bear—she didn't need her mother to remind her of it.

Bear grabbed her hand and turned her around to face him. "Hey," he said, putting a long finger under her chin and lifting her head until she had no choice but to look up at him. "I'm not the least bit offended, though I'll admit my leg is a little sore where your father kept kicking me under the table."

She gasped. "What? But why—"

His eyes twinkled and a half grin tugged at the corner of his mouth. "I think he was trying to hit your mother, but my legs were in the way."

She sighed heavily. "Wonderful," she said with a miserable eye-roll. "My mother all but accuses you of contracting sexually transmitted diseases from international prostitutes and my dad kicks you all through dinner."

He grinned. "It's fine, Veda," he assured her. "They're just worried about you. They want you to settle down with some nice boy from Hydrangea. And instead, you're seeing me. Or pretending to see me," he corrected, a slight flush creeping over his neck. "They just got you back. I can see why they would be concerned."

"Be that as it may, putting you through that interrogation was uncalled for. No more dinners with my parents," she said.

"Only if that's what you want," he told her. "I honestly don't mind." He grinned. "I'd endure a lot for real mashed potatoes and gravy. I don't get a lot of home-cooked meals."

No, she supposed he didn't. There were so many things she took for granted, Veda realized. "If we can get my kitchen and living room things moved in tonight, then I will happily make you mashed potatoes and gravy." And there was still his birthday celebration to plan.

"I don't see any reason why we can't get done tonight.

asked Mark, Ella's delivery boy, to be here at seven to help me with the furniture."

She smiled and held up a pair of keys. "And I've got Dad's truck. As I said, I really don't have a lot of furniture. A small dinette, a couch, a couple of chairs, a few bookcases and an old steamer trunk."

He jerked his head toward the birdcage. "What about her? Are we moving her tonight?"

Odette squawked and rattled her bell with her beak. "If you've ever financed a tattoo...you might be a redneck."

Bear's eyes widened and a bark of laughter erupted from his throat. "Wow," he said. "She's really got the accent down, doesn't she? And the inflection. It's perfect." He shook his head wonderingly, his golden eyes crinkling at the corners. "That's really incredible."

"It is," Veda agreed. "But it's a little unnerving when she does it at three in the morning."

"I imagine so," he said, watching the bird preen her feathers.

"I really shouldn't move her until all of the painting is done and the apartment has aired out. But once it's done, I think she'll like looking down over the square. There will always be something for her to watch. I know she gets lonely. She's used to being around people."

He turned to look at her once more and she was struck anew at just how perfect he was, how thoroughly masculine and handsome. She loved the clean angle of his jaw, the curiously vulnerable skin beneath it. A tiny breath shuddered out of her lungs as she imagined licking that skin, tasting it against her tongue.

"Have you ever thought about getting her a friend?" Bear asked, interrupting her preoccupation.

"I have, actually," Veda said, struggling to focus. "Er... once we're fully settled here I'm going to start looking for a companion for her." She smiled drolly and heaved a small sigh. "And then I'll have double the redneck and bunion jokes, plus whatever vocabulary the new bird comes with."

"Ah," he said. "I didn't think about that." He hummed under his breath. "You know that your mother can see right into the living room of this house, right?"

"What? No, I—" She peered around him and inhaled sharply as she watched her mother dart away from the back-door window. "Oh, for the love of—" She jerked the curtains closed, humiliated all over again.

"I know it's a pain in the ass, but be glad they worry, Veda. Be glad you have someone who cares about you."

It was a matter-of-fact comment, one delivered with very little inflection and yet she heard the sadness all the same. Her heart ached for him, longed to tell him that someone did—and would—worry about him. That, despite the fact that they'd spent more than a decade apart, she'd always cared for him. He'd always owned a little part of her. Whether she'd ever been truly aware of it or not, he'd been the stick every other guy had been measured against.

Though she'd been annoyed at her mother for asking Bear all those questions, a part of her had been thankful because a lot of them were ones she'd wanted to ask herself, but hadn't yet summoned the courage.

For instance, she'd had no idea that he'd gone into systems engineering while in college or that he'd just completed his fourth tour of duty in Afghanistan. She hadn't known that he'd lost a good friend last year when a roadside bomb had detonated alongside his convoy or that Bear himself had been shot two years ago. In the shoulder, he'd said, because he was such a big target. She doubted his mother had ever known, much less sent him a get well card or anything else.

Be glad you have someone who cares about you, he'd said. She was. And by the time he left at the end of the week,

Bear Midwinter was going to know that the people of this town cared about him.

And that she did, too.

Two HOURS LATER, wearing yoga pants and a tank top, her hair pulled up into a ponytail, Veda was removing books from a large plastic tote and loading them into bookshelves. Because she was the most efficient, organized person he'd ever met, it had taken barely any time at all to locate the boxes that held the items she'd needed for the kitchen and living room. Everything had been color-coded with dots and stacked accordingly in her parents' detached garage.

Furthermore, living in a small New York apartment had given her a minimalist attitude. She had everything that she needed, but very little of it. The less she had to take care of, the better, she'd said. "I don't want to be one of those people who are constantly worried about 'stuff,'" she told him. "I want to enjoy my downtime, not spend it taking care of things. The more you have, the more there is to do."

He'd never really thought of it like that, but had instantly agreed with her. His mother had been forever buying more, cluttering up the apartment.

Having moved all the furniture where Veda wanted it, he'd begun looking through her artwork and various pictures. She had several Degas prints—of ballerinas, of course—and a couple of black-and-whites of herself en pointe, in costume, on stage. He held one of those now and…mercy.

The angle of her head, the graceful line of her neck, the expression on her face. She was exquisite. Utterly, heart-stoppingly perfect. He wished he'd seen her dance, Bear thought. He wished—

"What are you looking at?" she asked, shooting him a quizzical look over her dainty shoulder.

Caught gawking, he smiled sheepishly and turned the

photo around. "You," he said. "You're beautiful." The words seemed inadequate, but it was the best he could come up with at the moment.

A creamy rose spread under her skin and she lowered her lashes. "Thank you. A woman in the audience took it," she said. "She sent the picture to the theater because she couldn't find an address for me. She said she thought she'd captured something special and she wanted me to have it."

He looked at it again—hell, couldn't stop looking at it—and felt some bizarre emotion wing through his rapidly tightening chest. "I'd have to agree with her. You're...art," he said, for lack of anything more clever, and chuckled nervously under his breath.

She smiled, evidently pleased with his inane comment. "That's what ballet is," she said. "It's art in motion."

"Where do you want this?" he asked.

"On top of this bookshelf, if you don't mind." She swallowed as she watched him set it in place. "I love that picture," she said. "I can look at it and know, in that moment, I was doing everything absolutely right."

In this moment, it was hard to imagine her doing anything wrong. The lamplight glowed against her cheek, illuminating the pale golden highlights in her hair and casting the other side of her face in stark relief. She had a tiny freckle just under her right eye that he'd never noticed before and the slightest dimple in her little chin. She moved with a gracefulness and economy of movement that was nothing short of mesmerizing and, though he didn't know what kind of perfume she was wearing—something floral with musky undertones—it was driving him insane. He wanted to breathe her in and eat her up. Slide his nose along the smooth column of her throat and get drunk on her skin.

With a satisfied sigh, she placed the last book on the shelf—Shakespeare's classics—and then started to stand.

He offered her a hand up and felt a tingling shoot up the backs of his legs and settle in his groin as her fingers clasped his. A startled flash lit her gaze at the contact and he knew she'd felt it, too.

Thank God.

"I can't believe you got all of this done today," she said, her gaze darting to his. "At the rate you're going, you'll be finished long before the weekend."

Because he couldn't think of a valid reason to continue clinging to her fingers, he reluctantly released her hand. "I doubt it," he said. "Even if I finish up here, I've still got the studio to work on."

She made her way to the fridge and pulled out a couple of beers, then made the return trek and handed him one. At some point, she'd hooked up her stereo, docked her iPod and currently a bluesy folk song he'd never heard but instantly liked was playing through the speakers. "So you're planning on staying in Hydrangea until you have to return to base?"

Her voice was light, almost casual, and yet he detected an undercurrent to the question that suggested his answer was much more important than she'd have him believe. Interesting. He dropped onto the couch and took a draw from the beer. "I am," he said. He had nowhere else to go, after all. His friends were still on vacation and it was too late to join them now, even if he'd wanted to. Which he didn't.

"Good," she said, taking the spot next to him. She grinned, her smile soft and sexy around the edges. "I'd hate for you to miss the Fried Festival."

"My life would be incomplete," he drawled, suddenly bone-tired. He felt fatigue pull at his lids and blinked sleepily.

"You know it," she told him, chuckling. She looked around the loft, appreciating the finished product, and nodded. "I think I'm going to like it here. It feels right."

It did, he had to agree. She'd chosen a warm yellow for the

kitchen and living room and the color was equally bright and welcoming. Her furniture wasn't new, but it was comfortable, made to be used. Oddly enough, he felt more at home in her space here in the loft than he ever had when it had belonged to his mother.

He gestured toward the music with his bottle before taking another drink. "Who is this?"

"The Civil Wars," she said. "They're good, aren't they?"

He nodded. "They are. I like this song."

"It's called 'Poison and Wine.' It's one of my favorites. The music sort of just winds around you, doesn't it?"

"Mmm-hmm."

She was quiet for a moment and when he opened his eyes, she was staring at him, an odd look on her face. Some unreadable emotion lurked in her gaze along with something else, something he recognized—longing.

"It's late," she breathed, pushing hastily to her feet. "I'd better get going."

In the time it had taken Bear to realize that she was bolting, she'd already grabbed her purse and keys and made it to the door. She paused, her hand on the knob, then swore and turned around…right into him.

She squeaked, then stumbled back and looked up. She moistened her lips and smiled. "Same time tomorrow night? I'll cook."

He slid a finger down the side of her face and felt her shudder, her breath catch. "A smudge of dirt," he lied, just wanting to touch her.

She offered another wobbly smile. "Oh. Thanks."

"Good night, Veda," Bear told her, his gaze purposely lingering on her mouth.

She blinked drunkenly, licking her lips. "'Night, Bear. I'll kiss you tomorrow."

"Come again?"

She squeezed her eyes tightly shut. "I'll see you tomorrow. See you," she repeated, and with another adorably muttered curse, she turned the knob and darted through the door.

Bear grinned. If it was up to him—and one way or another, it would be—then she'd do both.

9

"I HEARD HE'S working in her bedroom today," Veda heard Tina Charles tell someone in the grocery aisle next to her. "Harris was going on and on to someone about the particular shade of pink she'd chosen for her room and how he was certain Veda had some sort of gift for interior design."

"Well, if she's using Bear Midwinter as an accessory, then we certainly can't fault her taste, can we?" Mandy replied, laughing at her own joke.

"I could think of a thousand different ways to put his fine ass to work in my bedroom," Tina told her. "And none of them would involve a paintbrush."

Veda rounded the corner and arched a brow at both women. "Don't knock it until you've tried it, girls. In the right hands a paintbrush can be a—" she gave a delicate shudder "—beautiful thing."

Honestly, Veda thought, if they were going to talk about her, then she might as well give them something to talk about. And if it made them green with envy and netted her a little satisfaction in the process, then all the better. To be fair, Tina had always thought she was better than everyone else and had looked down her nose at the majority of their class—she was just like that. Mandy, on the other hand, had been like that as well, but with a cruel streak to boot. She'd had a keen way of sensing someone's weakness and exploiting that weakness, just for the fun of it.

With Veda, it had always been her height.

In retrospect, being petite was a good thing. But until her breasts and hips had come along—and, admittedly, she'd been a late bloomer—she'd looked more like a young boy than a teenage girl. As a result, Mandy had never failed to make some sort of comment about her flat chest, often telling people that a two-by-four had more dimension than she did. And she'd called her "Vern" instead of Veda. Later, after Veda had developed, Mandy had spread the rumor that Veda stuffed her bra and was constantly pulling tissues out of her pocket and wagging them at Veda.

She'd been a mean-spirited, small-minded bitch, Veda thought, and for the first time in her life, she had something that Mandy desperately wanted—Bear.

Of course, she didn't really have him, Veda thought as she selected a bunch of asparagus, but that was neither here nor there. Mandy and Tina both thought she did and that was all that mattered.

Furthermore, despite the fact that they hadn't had an audience last night and there'd been no one to "perform" for, there was no mistaking the hungry gleam in Bear's eyes or the resulting quiver that resounded through her sex. Sweet heaven. When he looked at her like that, stared at her mouth as though he wanted to devour her, well…she wanted to let him.

She'd wanted to do more than let him last night, as a matter of fact, but something had made her bolt instead. She suspected it was self-preservation, brought about by her mother's interference, and exacerbated by the fact that, if they stopped pretending, whatever this was between them would morph into something more, something that would make her want the one thing she knew she could never fully have—Bear.

It had taken her mother the better part of forty-five minutes, but the one thing she'd wanted her daughter to hear was that Bear had never considered making Hydrangea his permanent home. She'd asked him leading questions about the military, his career and where he saw himself in ten years. Though he'd been a bit taken aback by the last question, he'd answered with a simple shrug and a "Who knows? Wherever the military sends me, I suppose."

In other words, he'd never considered an alternate path, a different course, one that would provide a permanent home and roots in a community.

It was sad, really, because if anyone in the world needed a permanent home more desperately than Bear Midwinter, she'd certainly never met them.

"Afternoon, Veda," Ms. Ella said, nodding at the various groceries in her cart. Her eyes twinkled with knowing humor. "Making dinner this evening, are you?"

Veda nodded, nervously tucking a strand of hair behind her ear. She hoped like hell the paintbrush comment wouldn't make it back to Ella Johnston's ears. Oh, hell. Or her mother's, for that matter. "Yes, ma'am, I am."

"Well, you know what they say," she said. "A way to a man's heart is through his stomach." She leaned in and winked at her. "Of course, I've always found the path behind his zipper to be much more expedient."

Veda nearly choked on her tongue.

Ms. Ella nodded primly and pushed her cart on down the aisle, leaving Veda to wonder if the older woman had just suggested that instead of making a meal for Bear, she should make one of him.

BECAUSE HE'D KNOWN VEDA WANTED to move his mother's old iron bed into what used to be his room, Bear had spent the bulk of yesterday working there. His mother had painted the walls a deep plum—almost purple—and between the difficult-to-cover shade and the various dings and dents and nail holes she'd failed to spackle before applying that ghastly shade, it had taken him much longer than he'd anticipated to get it done.

He had, though, and when he finished, he'd moved the iron bed in so that he could start work on the master bedroom today. Veda had been pleased, but oddly nervous last night when she'd come over. She'd made a great meal, had done a few things around the loft—hung pictures, rearranged some bric-a-brac, hung curtains—but, citing being the official "taste-tester" for her mother's entry into the Fried Festival, she hadn't lingered as she had the night before. He wasn't altogether certain what had happened and, though she'd ultimately left, he could tell it had been reluctantly.

He'd been irrationally disappointed to see her go. He'd spent the day listening to her teach the kids downstairs, hearing the various music below his feet and somehow, just knowing that she was close had made him happier than he could recall in recent memory.

He liked the smooth cadence of her voice, the way she encouraged the girls. After listening to his mother scream and shout for years, Veda's approach was unbelievably different. And much better. While she might miss performing—and he sincerely hated that she wouldn't be able to do that anymore, at least at the level she was used to—he thought she made an excellent teacher.

Oddly enough, both his mother and Veda had been put into the same situation—forced out of their chosen career paths—and yet they'd reacted so differently. His mother's self-preservation skills had kicked in, but she'd felt robbed and became bitter. Veda, on the other hand, had given herself a little time to mourn her thwarted plans, but then immediately embraced the new one with determination and enthusiasm.

Veda, unlike his mother, was determined to be happy.

Furthermore, though he wasn't altogether sure if it was her mother's interrogation the other night over dinner or Veda's later admission that she'd never had a backup plan in the event that she couldn't dance anymore, but Bear had been thinking about what he'd do if he ever left the military. In all honesty, other than going out in a body bag, he'd never thought about it at all.

He'd wanted to join the military—to be a Ranger, specifically—ever since his junior year in high school when the local recruiter had come around. He'd listened to the man talk about his brothers in arms, being part of something bigger than himself, fighting for the greater good, the camaraderie, the sense of purpose shared by like-minded men and Bear had known then that the military would be the place for him.

And it had. He'd never regretted the career choice. He'd made lifelong friends and was proud of his service. But, for the first time in his life, being back here in Hydrangea as an adult—not just a man-child on the verge of maturity—he couldn't help but wonder if he'd missed the opportunity to have a different life, one that included a wife, children, a sense of community.

He'd watched a dad and daughter leave Veda's studio yesterday, her small hand tucked in his, her tutu glittering with sparkles, and a startling ache had settled in Bear's chest. In a flash of insight, he realized that he'd been so busy protecting his country that he'd never gotten a chance to have what it offered.

And until he came back to Hydrangea, with Veda and Ms. Ella and Harris and even Nancy, who'd been so kind to him, he'd never realized he might have wanted it after all.

It was madness, Bear told himself. It was this place, these people, being back here that was making him second-guess the life he'd chosen, the path he'd set upon. He was due back at Fort Benning in two days' time, he realized with an unhappy start. He had another six months before his current contract was up and already the powers that be were offering him re-up incentives. The only reason he hadn't signed the necessary paperwork was because he'd been arranging his visit here, making sure that his leave went through.

To see a mother who'd put some of his baby pictures in the "Salvation Army" pile, Bear thought bitterly, as well as a single photo of a man he suspected was his father. The picture had been torn, then taped back together and staring at it was like looking into a mirror. The man had been tall, like Bear, with wavy, tawny hair and pale brown eyes. Only a first name—Charlie—had been written on the back.

It was more than he'd ever dared hope to learn and was, ultimately, enough. He had a face and a name now. That was all he'd ever really wanted.

"Bear?"

He turned to find Veda behind him, a concerned line between her brows.

"Sorry," he said, setting the paint roller aside. "I didn't hear you."

"I was going to get something for lunch and thought you might want to take a break," she said, hooking her finger toward the door. She glanced around the master bedroom, seemingly pleased with the way it was turning out. "This looks good."

He nodded, poked his tongue in his cheek. "As well as it can for being pink."

She sent him a playful glare. "It's not pink. It's sheer rose, almost white really."

"Only if white is pink," he said, setting the roller aside. "I should be finished in an hour or so, and then I'm going to put the new fixtures in the bathroom and make sure that outlet is working by the sink. Once I'm done, I think that will complete everything on the loft list, right?"

She blinked, seemingly startled that he was almost finished. A strange expression—desperation, maybe?—briefly crossed her face. She pushed her hand through her hair, tugging the silky strands away from her face. "Er...yeah," she said, eyes widening significantly. "I hadn't realized that you were..." She blew out a breath and shook herself. "That's wonderful. Fantastic," she said, although her tone didn't support the adjective.

He knew exactly how she felt.

"We should be able to move the rest of your things in tonight," he told her. "If I leave the windows open for the rest of the day, do you think the room will be aired out enough to bring Odette?"

She'd been looking at a place on the floor, but at his question, she seemed to jerk to attention. "Yes, I think so," she told him. "She could spend the night here with you and keep you company."

Bear rubbed a hand over the back of his neck and smiled at her. He hesitated. Oh, what the hell. He had two days left. Two measly days. "Actually, I don't see why we all couldn't spend the night here. You'll have your room and I can take the spare. Of course, if the idea makes you uncomfortable, then I understand, but strictly speaking—"

"The only thing that makes me uncomfortable about it is the talk that's bound to ensue. Hydrangea's a small town."

Bear grinned. "Veda, they're already talking," he said. He feigned a frown. "Women keep looking at me with these disturbing little grins—like they're privy to something I'm not—and telling me that their paintbrushes need cleaning." He glanced up at her and noticed her face had gone beet-red. That was the thing about blondes—when they blushed, they really blushed. "Veda? Are you all right?"

She cleared her throat. "What? No, I'm fine," she said, giving her head a little shake.

"Do you know what they're talking about? What is it exactly that I'm supposed to be so good at with a paintbrush?" He had his suspicions, of course, but was enjoying needling her.

She blinked innocently, but had never looked more guilty. "No idea," she said, blowing out a breath.

He laughed. "Liar."

"How do you know I'm lying?"

"The tops of your ears turn pink."

She inhaled and reached for one of the offending ears. "That's only because I'm embarrassed," she said. "It doesn't mean I'm lying."

He'd just bet she turned pink all over. The thought made a sizzle of heat zip into his groin and he felt his dick twitch in response. Pink, creamy flesh, naked and writhing beneath him... "But you are, aren't you?"

She looked away and swore, then bit her lip. "I might have mentioned to a couple of people that we've done more than just paint with one of your brushes," she said. "That we might use them in the bedroom as a kind of—"

"Sex toy?" he supplied helpfully.

She winced, casting him a look beneath a sweep of lashes. "Possibly, yes."

He chuckled and quirked a disbelieving brow. "And you're worried about spending the night under the same roof after you've put that image in people's heads?" He grunted. "No doubt the whole town thinks that the new shower rod I put in the bathroom is your new dance pole."

"You got a new shower rod? That wasn't on the list."

"It was rusty."

"Oh." Her cell phone beeped, indicating she'd gotten a new text message, and she checked the display. Whatever was on there made her scowl. "You know what?" she remarked in a particularly chipper tone. "You're right. People are going to think whatever the hell they want to. I'm ready to move in."

He suspected it was more a case of her wanting to move out of the carriage house and away from her mother, but whatever worked. He just wanted to spend more time with her. Breathe the same air.

Irrationally pleased, Bear smiled at her. "Good. Now let's go get that lunch you mentioned. I'll let you feed me and we'll really set the tongues to wagging."

She nodded, a smile playing over her lips. "Sounds like a plan."

It did...and he had a lot more where that idea had come from.

10

VEDA TUGGED the bedspread into place, then stood up and braced her hands on the small of her back and stretched. That was it, the last thing on the to-do list here in the house. Bear had gotten Mark to recruit a couple of his friends from the football team and, between the four of them, they'd moved Veda's bedroom furniture, the remaining linens for the bathroom, all of her clothes and Odette.

What would have taken several hours ultimately took only two. She was nothing short of amazed. Veda might be organized, but when it came to directing things in the most efficient manner, Bear definitely had her beat. She often glimpsed the soldier in him—the certain cock of his head, the way he continually scanned his surroundings, his attention to detail—but tonight she'd seen the leader, as well.

As much as she was thrilled that she'd finally be able to move into the loft—especially once she got her mother's I've-invited-Kenny-to-dinner-again text, which had propelled her to take the leap—there was a part of her that was sad, as well. Every item Bear ticked off the list put him that much closer to walking out of her life again. And she couldn't think about that without feeling like an elephant was sitting on her chest.

It was awful, terrifying even, because she knew—she'd

always known, hadn't she?—that she was never going to care about anyone else the way she did Bear Midwinter. She was never going to want a man more, she was never going to look at one and feel as deeply, need as wholly as she did when she was with him. He was warm and funny and good and every time he smiled, a little part of her soul sang. Why? Who knew? She sure as hell didn't. But Bear…something about Bear just did it for her. He always had.

"Veda?"

And then there was that voice—smooth, with a slightly rough finish. She turned and arched a brow. "Yes?"

"Do people still swim in Blue Water Creek?"

Of all the things he could have asked, that question hadn't even been on her radar. "I, uh…I don't know why they wouldn't. Why?"

He grinned at her, his golden eyes alight with mischief and something else, something almost…wicked. "I haven't been swimming in years," he said. "We've worked hard today and everything is done in here. We've earned a bit of a break, wouldn't you say?"

She hadn't been swimming in years, either, and no longer owned a suit. Of course, most bra-and-panty sets covered as much as the average two-piece so that really wasn't an issue. She smiled up at him, excitement curling like smoke through her. "You want to go swimming? Now?"

He nodded. "Now's good. You game?"

Veda shrugged, grinning. Why the hell not? "Sure," she said.

Ten minutes later, Bear pulled his rental car onto the small, graveled path that led to the deepest part of Blue Water Creek, where a bend in the flow created a natural pool of sorts, one that generations of Hydrangea residents had been coming to for years. He wheeled the car into a decent spot and climbed from behind the wheel. Veda had brought a quilt, a couple of towels and a cooler stocked with beer. A light breeze drifted over the moonlit water, tugging at the loose tendrils of hair around her face and she breathed in that sweet air, felt it loosen something inside of her.

This had been a brilliant idea. She shot Bear a look and told him as much.

"I'm glad you approve," he said, shrugging out of his shirt. His skin gleamed where the pale light touched it, casting his impressive frame in as much shadow as unearthly glow. His shoulders were even wider than she'd realized, heavily muscled, a masterful work of sinew, bone and vein. He stretched, shoving his hands through his hair, then straightened, and one hand dropped the snap at his shorts. Without the smallest hesitation, he popped the closure from its mate, his zipper whined in the sudden silence and he shucked his shorts and stepped out of them. For one mesmerizing instant she thought he'd stripped naked, but a closer look revealed he wore a pair of tight-fitting boxer shorts.

With a little quirk of his lips that told her he knew exactly what he was doing to her—and what she'd thought—he winked at her and headed into the water.

Feeling as if she was hot-and-embarrassed and hot-and-bothered all the time, Veda decided cooling off was definitely in order. She spread the blanket, kicked the flip-flops off her feet, then shrugged out of her T-shirt and shorts. She considered going behind a shrub to change, but he was going to see her anyway, so why bother? Her bra and panties were a nude shade, accented with sheer lace. She knew she looked naked and had the privilege of watching Bear's mouth drop open when he caught sight of her. He went comically still.

She reached up and tugged the ponytail holder from her hair and then shook it out before starting toward the water. She knew she wouldn't pass for a Baywatch girl, but there was a certain level of satisfaction in Bear's reaction all the same.

She waded in and let the water cool her heated skin. Beau was several feet from her, floating on his back, the water lapping over those wonderful shoulders, tightening the masculine nipples on his chest. She was hit with the sudden urge to taste one, to lick it, bite it.

She dunked herself, counted to five, then came back up again. He was right in front of her, all six and a half feet of hard-muscled, masculine perfection. Veda smothered a whimper.

"You startled me," she said, staring up at him.

His eyes drifted over her bare shoulders, dipped down into the deep V between her breasts and lingered over her taut nipples. Despite the heat, gooseflesh skittered over her skin.

"You went under and didn't come back up."

She couldn't look away from him, held nearly breathless a captive of that amber gaze. "I was cooling off."

He stared hungrily at her mouth and his voice lowered an octave. "Did it work?"

She swallowed, balled her hands at her sides to keep from reaching out and tracing the muscles on his chest, sliding her fingertips along the edges of his pecs, over every bump and ridge of his abdomen. "Not particularly," she said.

Need screamed along every nerve ending, vibrating between them like some living, breathing thing. She watched the pulse beat at the base of his neck, the muscles in his throat work as he swallowed. A rivulet of water slid next to his mouth and she was jealous of that little bit of moisture because it clung to his skin the way she wanted to.

"No one is here, Veda," he said, his tone low, almost foggy.

She frowned uncertainly.

"There is no audience." He reached up and slipped a finger along her cheek, the gentle touch rocketing through her. Her breath caught and she bit her lip. "No one to put on a show for. Just you and me and the moonlight." He bent down and d his nose alongside hers, his mouth hovering just out of ich. She could taste him already, could feel the heat lick-g between them. "Here's a secret," he whispered, his breath ining against her lips. "I haven't been pretending at all. It's been real to me."

Her gaze tangled with his, then she melted against him d kissed him the way she'd been dying to do all week. He is hot and hard and wet and he tasted like sin and salva-n, like beer and chocolate—no doubt one of the stars Ms. la had given him—and she wrapped her arms around him, shing her hands into the short hair along his nape, feeling s muscles tense and bunch against her fingers.

He groaned low in his throat, lifted her up and licked a path ing her neck, his clever tongue tracing the delicate shell of r ear. She shuddered against him, felt his big hands settle both sides of her ass and squeeze, and she responded in nd by wrapping her legs around his waist. She framed his ce with her hands once more and brought his mouth back hers for another frantic kiss. It was deep and dark and pur-seful, a mating of mouths. She sucked his tongue into her outh, mimicking another sort of oral play and his moan of easure vibrated through her. She could feel the length of him essing high against her sex and that simple nudge tripped on switch inside of her, making her mindless with want, sperate with need.

She slid her hands all over him, savoring his warm, wet in against her palms, and continued to feed at his mouth d rock herself shamelessly against him. Every pulse beat mmered in her blood, resonated in her womb. He started alking her toward the bank, as though she weighed noth-g, his big hands still on her ass.

He carefully laid her on the quilt, then slid a hand down r middle and followed the path with his tongue. His hot eath fanned over her skin, over her aching nipples, and he

sucked one pouting peak through the wet, thin fabric of
bra. A second later, he'd popped the front closure, baring
to him, and then he tasted her once more, rasping his tong
against her, laving her as she'd thought about doing to hi
She bucked against him, looking for that divine weight, t
one true thing that would make the madness recede. A
then his fingers were on her, beneath her panties, stroki
the heart of her.

Veda gasped and tightened around him, then reached do
and palmed him through the boxers. He was long and ha
and thick and…damn, she just wanted him.

All of him.

She worked the boxers down over his lean hips and to
him in hand, then stroked the silky skin atop the head
his penis. He jerked against her, exhaling a shaken brea
"Veda," he said warningly, his voice harsh.

Empowered, she smiled and touched him again.

He swore. "Woman, I—"

A thought struck and she almost whimpered. "Please t
me you have a condom in your shorts," she said, leaning f
ward and kissing the side of his neck.

His chuckle was low and wicked. "I do," he said.
waited, suckled the other breast, dallied between her thig
until she thought she might explode. Or die. At this point
ther one would be a relief. "Do you want me to put it on?"

"Yes," she said, arching up against him. She could feel t
climax building in the back of her womb, circling closer a
closer to that mystical edge that would send her into conv
sions of delight. Seconds later he was sheathed and nud
ing thickly between her folds. Moonlight gilded his glorio
body and she slid her hands over his chest and thought, *Mi*
Then she moved them over his tight belly and thought, *Mi*
And then she arched back and grabbed his ass and thoug
Mine, mine, mine.

His gaze tangled with hers, then he bent forward and pressed his lips to hers, slid his tongue into her mouth and slid the rest of himself into her. Veda inhaled sharply as sensation bolted through her. Her vision blackened around the edges and every cell in her body sang with some unnamed, unrecognizable joy.

Bear swore and drew back, his entire body quaking. "Damn, but you're small. Am I hurting you? Are you—"

Veda tightened around him and she heard him suck air through his teeth. "Does that feel good?"

"Yes," he hissed.

She bent forward, wrapped her legs more tightly around him and licked a path up the side of his neck. "So do you," she said. "All of you. Don't worry, I won't break…but I'm sure as hell looking forward to falling apart."

Bear chuckled, withdrew and then sank back into her. He did it over and over again, slowly at first, stoking the fire that burned within her, then faster and faster. In and out, harder and harder, until nothing mattered but the pleasure of their joined bodies. She bucked beneath him, met him thrust for thrust, then tightened around him, desperate to hold on to him, to keep him inside of her.

She felt the release crest low in her sex, then suddenly the ground seemed to give way beneath her back and she was free-falling through sensation, clinging to him as a long, keening cry tore from her throat and brought tears to her eyes.

Her release triggered his, as well, and she felt him go rigid above her, every muscle in his body locked down tight. He buried himself in her as far as he could go and held steady, letting the orgasm rush through him. His big shoulders shook, his arms quaked and his lips were on hers, kissing her, tasting her, making her feel wanted, needed, God help her, loved even. There was a note of desperation, of affection in his kiss that was somehow more profound than anything else and it shook her to the core.

He'd rattled her very foundation. And Veda knew she'd never be the same again.

11

BEAR AWOKE THE NEXT MORNING with a soft mound of breast beneath his hand and a lovely rump pressed against his groin. Veda's hair was inches from his face and the scent of her shampoo, something fruity and warm, hung in the air between them. The first fingers of dawn were clawing above the horizon, casting beams of light against the wall and, try as he might, he couldn't think of a single morning that had ever topped this one. Contentment saturated every cell in his body, made him feel sluggish and happy.

Last night had been… He struggled to find the right words and realized there weren't any. Last night had defied description, was beyond anything in his understanding. How could he understand it when he had no frame of reference for these feelings?

When it came to experience, though, he wasn't a man-whore by any means and had never, despite what Veda's mother had thought, entertained a hooker, but Bear wasn't a novice. He'd lost his virginity in his early teens and had been having sex at regular intervals ever since. Sex was good, period, and he'd always liked it.

But what he'd felt with Veda last night went well beyond anything he'd ever experienced before. That first nudge into her tight little body had left him breathless, irrationally terrified and thrilled. And when she'd arched up, welcomed him in and tightened around him, that single contraction had flipped some sort of emotional trigger for him. He'd gone from simply being mindless with need to having to have her. Her every sigh, every mewl of pleasure, every slide of her skin against his, every touch of her hands against his body had enflamed him more than anything he'd ever felt before. She'd become his east and west, his moon and stars, the very air he'd breathed.

God help him, his home.

And the day after tomorrow, he was leaving her.

She stirred beside him, stilled for just a moment and then, smiling sleepily, rolled to face him. "Morning," she said, her voice rusty from sleep. "Happy birthday."

He blinked, surprised, and then chuckled and pressed a kiss to her forehead. "Thank you."

"How's it going so far?" she asked, turning more fully against him. Her breath fanned against his neck and her hand snaked around his middle and drifted slowly up over his back. He hardened, jerked against her and he felt her smile, the barest upturn of her cheek.

"No complaints," he told her, pulling her more firmly against him.

She rolled on top of him, her naked sex slipping over his. Leaning forward, she pressed a kiss below his ear. He shuddered at the contact. "I'm protected and clean," she said, her voice low. "You?"

"As a whistle," he told her, wincing with pleasure as she slid over him again, coating him in her essence.

"In that case—" she leaned back, pressed her hands against his chest, then rose up and impaled herself on him, sinking degree by degree, taking him into her hot, little body "—I'm going to give you your present a little early."

Bear grasped her hips, bent forward and pulled a rosy nipple into his mouth, giving him the pleasure of feeling her tighten around him, as though there were some sort of reciprocating chord between the two. He did it again and her feminine muscles clamped around him once more. Then she rose up and sank again, riding him slowly, deliberately, her sweetly flared hips rocking above him. Her musky scent swirled around him, drugging him, as he fed at her breasts and traced the fluted line of her spine with his thumbs.

She leaned farther back, taking more and more of him inside of her, and she upped the tempo, her ministrations growing more frantic, increasingly desperate. Her breath left her in little puffs and then her eyes drifted shut, as though the weight of desire required too much effort to keep them open. The morning sun filtered through the sheer curtains, bathing the room with light and the closer he came to release, the brighter the room grew. He felt the orgasm gather in the back of loins and held on tight while she rode him harder and harder. A little mewling cry as well as the more determined drag and draw between their bodies told him she was close. He reached between them, found the kernel of sensation nestled high at the top of her sex and stroked it once, twice, three times.

Predictably, she shattered.

So did he…and the light that burst into the room at that moment damn nearly blinded him.

Breathing heavily, she collapsed against his chest, her heart beating frantically against his, a steady tattoo of feeling, sensation, longing and contentment.

A thought struck and he chuckled softly.

She drew back and stared at him. "What's that laugh for?" she asked, a brow arched in suspicion.

"That's twice now and we haven't used a paintbrush yet," he said. "I hope you're not disappointed."

She grinned. "Not in the slightest. You are a sex toy," she said, kissing his chest. "Who needs a paintbrush?"

He laughed again and absently doodled on her back, drawing lazy circles. "I don't know whether to be flattered or offended," he teased. "I'm not sure I like the idea of being a sex object."

She snorted. "Yeah, right. You know you're hot."

Another chuckle bubbled up his throat. "I don't know about that, but I know you're good for my ego."

She snuggled more firmly against him. "Want me to make you feel even better?"

He hummed contentedly. "How so?"

"By telling you a secret."

Intrigued, he played along. "Whose secret?"

"Mine."

"Yes, definitely. This sounds like something I need to know."

He felt her hesitate. Then she said, "I had a huge crush on you when I was younger. Like, massive. I thought about you for years after you moved away. 'Pined' according to my mother. That's why she was so unhappy about us dating. She was afraid I'd fall for you all over again and be devastated when you left."

Bear didn't know what he'd expected her to say, but this certainly wasn't it. He swallowed, touched, honored. "I had no idea," he said. He stilled. "Is that why you threw up on me? Because I made you nervous?"

"Yes," she said, her voice wry. "Thanks for bringing that up."

"Sorry." He chuckled. "That's actually preferable to me thinking I made you sick."

She kissed his chest again. "I think we've established that you have a different effect on me now."

"I like this one better," he told her, holding her more tightly.

"Come to think of it, you did follow me around a lot," he remarked.

"That's because I adored you, fool. When I found out that you were coming back to town, that I was going to see you again, I was an absolute wreck. You were The Guy, you know? You've always been The Guy."

Unaccountably, his heart had begun to pound and his mouth had gone dry.

"I was afraid of making a fool of myself, but then you came up with the let's-pretend-to-date idea and that got me off the hook." She drew back, looked at him. "You aren't the only one who hasn't been pretending." Her gaze searched his, that unreadable emotion that he'd gotten used to seeing in her pretty green eyes glowing like a beacon. "I think you're pretty damned great, you know that?"

"I could say the same to you."

She sighed theatrically and settled against him again. "I keep waiting," she said.

Suddenly nervous, Bear smiled and searched for the right words. "I've never met anyone like you, Veda. You make me think about things I've never considered before."

"Like what?"

"Like an alternate career path. I admire what you've done here. Life dealt you a blow and you hit it right back. You didn't flinch. You blazed a new trail. That's brave."

"I've…never thought of it like that before."

"Well, you should. You should be proud of yourself."

She gave him a squeeze. "We both should, Bear. Not many people could have had the upbringing you had and been anything less than a basket case." She hesitated. "I know I shouldn't say this, but I'm going to because I think you need to hear it. Your mother was awful…most particularly, to you. She never showed you an ounce of affection, of real love. She never looked further than her own needs and yet somehow, you turned into a wonderful, honorable, good man. Ask anyone," she said. "They'll tell you. All of Hydrangea thinks you hung the moon." She giggled. "Hell, Ms. Ella all but told me to sleep with you, that the fastest way to your heart was behind your zipper."

Bear felt his eyes widen and he gasped. "She didn't."

"She did," Veda insisted. "You could have knocked me over with a feather."

"I don't know why I'm surprised," he said. "She's the one who included condoms in the care package she sent over."

Veda leaned back and stared at him. "Oh, God. Really? That feels almost…dirty."

He felt his lips twitch. "Yeah…but you're glad she did, aren't you?"

Her twinkling gaze searched his. "That easy to read, am I?"

"I'm getting better at it."

"I don't know whether to be happy or alarmed."

Then that made two of them, Bear thought. Because at the moment, he was as happy as he'd ever been in his life. And it scared him to death.

WELL, SHE'D LAID IT ALL OUT on the line, Veda thought as she waited for Bear to try one of Harris's fried squash puppies that evening. She'd told him that he was The Guy, that she'd been so nervous about seeing him again that she'd thrown up and that she'd never been pretending. That she'd always wanted him. She hadn't added the "and always will," but it had been implied.

Now, hours later, with the minor repairs made to the studio and the Fried Festival in full swing, they were less than a day away from his leaving, a fact that neither one of them had dared mention. Still, it hung between them like a lingering stench.

He slung an arm around her shoulder and she smiled, wishing the sensation wasn't so bittersweet. "Those squash puppies were good," he said. "Did you try one?"

Veda shook her head, catching her mother looking at her from across the square, a sad, resigned look on her face. "No," she told him. "I'm leaving room for the dessert category."

He inclined his head knowingly. "Right. The one your mother is entering. Have you tried her secret recipe?"

Her lips twisted. "Not since she found out we were seeing each other. She knows how close you are to Ella. She was afraid I'd slip up and say something to you and that you'd, in turn, tell Ella."

He looked down at her, his golden eyes wide in disbelief. "Seriously?"

She nodded once. "I told you this was a big deal."

He shook his head. "Sheesh. I believe you."

Hand in hand, they strolled around the festival, trying different recipes, laughing with various people who were only too glad to welcome them both back to the community. Inasmuch as she was able, Veda tried to stay in the moment, not fast forward ahead to what she knew was going to be the most horrible part of all this—watching him leave. Every time she thought about it, a lump swelled in her throat and a sense of dread crowded into her chest, making her sick with fear and nausea.

"You all right?" he asked as they waited for the final judging to commence and the winners to be announced. He squeezed her hand. "You're awfully quiet."

"Just eaten too much," she said, which was true, as well.

"Veda, Bear," Mandy said, strolling up with Tina, her sidekick, in tow. "Y'all look like you're having a wonderful time."

He tightened his hold on her and let his gaze drift slowly over her face. "We are," he said, not deigning to even look at Mandy.

Mandy's eyes hardened and she feigned a sympathetic wince. "How terrible tomorrow will be for you, then. Aren't you leaving? Or did I get the day wrong?" She tsked. "However will you survive, Veda?"

She felt him stiffen beside her and he finally turned to look at Mandy. "Well, considering she's got family here to love her until I get back, I think she's going to fare much better than I will. I'd rather walk in front of a firing squad tomorrow than leave her here, but going AWOL would net me an arrest warrant and a dishonorable discharge. Veda deserves better than that. When I come back, I want her to be proud of me."

Though she knew he was only saying those things to put Mandy in her place, Veda nevertheless wanted to believe them all the same. It almost hurt to hear his words, knowing they weren't true.

She summoned the required resolve, though, and nudged his shoulder. "I'll always be proud of you, Bear, no matter what. You ought to know that by now."

Something flashed in his gaze, but it passed too quickly for her to discern it. He bent and dropped a lingering kiss against her lips. "I know I should," he said. "But some things are harder to believe than others."

"Citizens and guests of Hydrangea," the mayor announced in ringing tones. "The time has come to name the Grease Master of this year's Fried Festival. We've had some tough competition, lots of new entries and the judges—who will no doubt need some antacids tonight—have had to make some hard decisions. But the fat's outta the fire now and it's time to get down to business."

"Boy, he really gets into this, doesn't he?" Bear asked. "I wonder how long he works on this speech."

Veda shushed him, hoping for her mother's sake that she managed to hang on to her title this year. Personally, the orange zest fritters had been her favorite, but she had no idea if that had been her mother's entry or not. The mayor awarded Harris's squash puppies runner-up in appetizer category and awarded first place to Reverend Morris for his zucchini parmesan sticks. Veda hadn't tried those, but thought they sounded good.

Category after category was called out until finally nothing but the dessert entries remained. The ladies of Hydrangea were on pins and needles, most especially her mom, who was standing as close to her father as she could without being surgically attached. Much like she and Bear were, Veda noted.

Come to think of it, her parents had always been especially close, and particularly affectionate. They were devoted to one another, finished each other's sentences and still held hands after all these years, which she'd thought was sweet.

But it was more than that, Veda realized now. They were in love. Truly, deeply, irrevocably in love…and that's what her mother wanted for her. Though she'd heard their story many, many times—the way her mother had practically driven away Dad's fiancée and somehow made her father wait for her to get out of high school—she'd only just now realized what that had really meant. Her dad was six years older than her mother and, according to her mom, she'd known from the time she was a little girl that they were made for each other.

Her mother had known that her dad should be hers the same way Veda had known that she'd loved Bear.

It was real for you, she'd said. And she knew, because she'd been through it herself. So why had she been so desperate to show her why Bear was wrong for her? Veda wondered. Why had she—

Ah.

Because, unlike her father, Bear had no intention of staying in Hydrangea. He was only here temporarily and her mother knew their relationship would either end with Veda's heart breaking or with her following Bear.

She just got you back, Bear had said.

And she'd just gotten him back. She didn't want him to leave, Veda thought, feeling emotion push into her throat again. She wanted him to stay with her. She wanted to wake up with him in the morning, his big body against hers, and go to sleep with him at night in the same manner. She wanted to see him across the breakfast table and lie in his lap while they watched movies. She wanted to take long walks while holding hands and talk about things that mattered and things that didn't. She wanted to fight and make up, to celebrate milestones, holidays and every mundane thing in between.

She just wanted him.

And she might as well want the moon, Veda thought, for all the good it was going to do her.

"And this year's winner of the dessert category and all around Grease Master is…Emmaline Hayes!" he shouted.

Veda jumped and whooped for her mom, who hurried toward the stage.

"Emmaline's entry this year was nothing short of mouth-watering. I had three of her orange zest fritters and thought I had died and gone to heaven." He handed her mother the trophy. "Tell us, Emmaline, what was your secret?"

Her mother grinned. "Now, Mayor, if I told you that, it wouldn't be a secret anymore, would it?"

The remark elicited a laugh from the crowd.

Ms. Ella strolled up next to them and huffed a breath. "Honestly, boy, I slipped you the chocolate stars and the condoms and you still couldn't find out for me what Emmaline was entering?"

Bear grinned. "Ella, I—"

"Oh, don't look so alarmed," she told him. "But if I'm the last to hear about your wedding, I'm cutting you off." And with that remark, she disappeared into the crowd.

Seemingly dumbstruck, Bear looked down at Veda. "Wedding," he repeated. He glanced around the assembled crowd, his gaze thoughtful, wondering, hopeful. Then he took a deep breath and found her gaze once more. "You know I have to leave tomorrow," he said. "But I don't want to. I want to stay here with you and build a life. A family. I want to have what your parents have. Honestly, I don't know how to do that— I was never equipped with the right example—but you had it. You can show me." He laughed, adorably terrified, but certain all the same. "I'm not sure how I'll earn a living, but I've got enough money put aside to take a little time to figure that out. I just know that I don't want to leave without making you mine, without knowing that you'll wait for me. That you're here for me."

Veda's eyes stung with emotion and she swallowed. "Bear, of course I'll wait—"

He took both of her hands in his and gave a gentle, meaningful squeeze as his gaze searched hers. "Marry me, Veda. Right here, right now. Reverend Morris is here, your parents are here, the whole damned town is here. There's plenty of food and a band, and we'll honeymoon tonight in your pink room while Odette complains about her corns and cracks Jeff Foxworthy jokes."

Veda chuckled, her pulse pounding so hard in her ears she could barely hear herself think. "Are you serious?" she said, casting a look around to see if anyone had overheard him. "Have you lost your mind?"

"No," he said. "I've lost something much more significant than that—my heart. It's yours. I might not have loved you as long as you've loved me, but make no mistake, I do love you. Marry me," he said again, his eyes twinkling. "Come on, Veda. You know you wanna," he cajoled. "We'll make Fried Festival history."

They would…and then they'd make their own history.

She nodded, thrilled and more than a little concerned about her sanity, then leaped up and wrapped her arms around him.

"Ella," he called, moving swiftly through the crowd. "You're going to hear it first...."

In short order Reverend Morris was rounded up, the band played the intro to the "Wedding March" and both Veda's father and mother gave her away. When the "I do's" were finished and the fritters and first dance were concluded, Bear picked up his bride and made for the loft to the sound of laughter, catcalls and applause. Harris, breathing heavily, hurried forward until he caught up with them.

"Here," he said, handing Bear a new paintbrush. "I thought you might need a new one."

Veda felt herself turn six shades of red. She and Bear shared a look and then broke into laughter.

For the record, they didn't need the paintbrush, but the whole town speculated about what they were doing with it for years to come. Particularly Tina and Mandy.

EMMALINE HAYES WATCHED HER NEW son-in-law carry her daughter across the square and felt her eyes mist with tears. "You see, Redmond," she said. "All's well that ends well. I knew things would turn out fine between them. I knew from the moment I watched them together that Bear was going to see the light."

Her husband shot her an indulgent smile. "Of course you did, dear."

See? This was what she loved about him. He knew when to lie to her.

"I don't know what you were so worried about," she continued lightly. "Aren't you glad we didn't interfere?"

He slung an arm over her shoulder and sighed. "Yes, I am."

"Having Ella slip them the condoms was a brilliant touch, don't you think?"

"I try not to think about that part of it, sweetheart. She is my daughter."

And now she was Bear's wife...Veda Midwinter. The woman she'd always wanted to be.

Mission accomplished, Emmaline thought. Now she could concentrate on getting that grandchild....

* * * * *

TAWNY
WEBER

WILD THING

To Brenda, who always sees the inner beauty, whether it's in a dog like Medusa or in one of my stories. Thanks for everything!

And to Rhonda, I'm totally grateful for the inspiration and laughter. And, of course, for the awesome stories you write.

1

"JOLENE, I'M A P.I. Not a puppy-retrieval service."

For just one second, Percy Graham visualized changing careers. Enthusiastic dogs with wagging tails, happy pet owners eager to greet their furry companions. Sure, maybe he'd get the occasional ankle biter, but that was probably better than being shot at.

He sighed. He was damn tired of being shot at. And cussed out. And failing.

All of which were becoming an irritating constant in his life lately. Ever since The Failure.

It was enough to give a guy a complex.

"Besides," he continued before his secretary could insist again that picking up a dog from the groomer's was a job requiring a licensed investigator. "I've got a plane to catch. Vacation, remember?"

"I know, sugar. You've got big decisions to make."

"Right," Percy murmured. The partnership. Wasn't taking on a partner the ultimate failure? It meant he couldn't make it alone. Even if he liked the guy he was considering, admired his work, it still meant giving up control.

"Just think about it. That's what this break is for, right?

You're falling apart at the seams. I swear, you keep up this pace and you're gonna ruin your health," Jolene said, her two-pack-a-day voice coming through his car's speaker in a loud rasp. "You're going too fast. You need to spend some time in front of the TV instead of all those hours you work chasing jobs, and maybe visit your momma instead of doing paperwork in the office on the weekends. That'd do you more good than flitting off to Bermuda for a week."

It'd definitely get him a fast pass to an early grave. At least, the weekends with his mother would.

"Jolene," Percy interrupted before she got to the inevitable dissection of his love life. It was something that'd always amused him before. But now it was just depressing. "What's the deal on the dog?"

He could almost hear her grin through the dash of his prized '67 Corvette. He couldn't say no to her, and she knew it. She'd probably already deposited the fee.

"It's a last-minute job. I didn't have the heart to say no. You handled a background check for this guy last year, did a few smaller jobs. With how bad things have been lately, I figured it'd be like good karma or something. You help him out by getting his dog then go catch your plane. When you get back, karma will have a bunch of new clients all lined up."

"I'm not sure that's how karma works," he muttered. Then again, what did he know? He wouldn't have said bad luck could grab hold and turn a guy's happy life upside down, yet it had. Ever since The Failure, he'd had nothing but, well, failures. It was like a chain reaction of suckiness.

Failed cases. Failed communications. Failed dates. Hell, it was getting so he was scared to take a woman to bed. Who knew what else might fail?

Yeah, he had to decide what to do about the partnership offer. Because while things were sucking right now, he did have a damn good rep in the business. Which was why he wanted—no, needed—this vacation. A change of scene, a chance to regroup, rethink and revive his libido, and he'd be good as new.

While he sat lost in thought, Jolene continued her verbal restructuring of his habits and despairing over his ever finding the right woman. Percy let the lecture wash right over him, focusing instead on traffic and the knots of stress wrapped around his spine. For a man who'd had life handed to him on a shiny platter, things had lately taken a turn toward Suckville. And he could pinpoint the exact moment they'd turned—the morning the sexiest woman he'd ever tasted had walked out, leaving him sleeping in the bed they'd spent hours in together.

It'd been his first. First time falling in love, first time getting dumped, first time feeling like a total failure. But like that stupid law-of-attraction stuff Jolene was always jabbering on about, one failure had drawn in another and another. And before long, he'd blown two cases in a row and his office had burned down.

"I'm on vacation," he interrupted when Jolene had reached the suggested-therapists portion of her lecture. "Give the case to Matthews. He wants this partnership. Let's see how he handles a spur-of-the moment job."

"No can do. Mr. Day wanted the best and that's you. You wouldn't have me lie to a client, would you? Especially one who's willing to pay this much money? It'll be easy. I texted you the address of the groomer. All you have to do is go in there and stage a rescue."

Rescue a dog from the groomer's? It smelled a little fishy to him.

"What's the real deal? Since when does a dog getting a haircut require a rescue mission?"

"Mr. Day is in the middle of an ugly divorce. He was

awarded custody of the dog but his soon-to-be ex-wife won't hand it over. Today it's the mutt's thrice-weekly grooming appointment, so he wants you to go over there and get it for him."

"Custody. Of a dog?"

"It's a really special dog."

"And he wants me to steal it?"

"It's legal," Jolene insisted. "He sent me the paperwork."

"This is what my career has come to?" he summed up, only a little bitter. All it took was one woman to dump him, and everything else went down the toilet.

"You'd be crazy to turn away from an easy-paying job right now, Percy. I do your books. I know these things. Just rescue our client's baby, drop it off here and I'll take care of everything else," Jolene commanded before he could argue more. Then, to make sure she got in the last word, she added just before she hung up, "And remember, don't shoot anyone."

"I haven't even fired my damn gun in three months," Percy groused to himself. The way his luck had been running, he'd been afraid he'd shoot himself in the foot. Jolene was right, though. He couldn't afford to turn away a quick and simple job.

Still, who the hell fought over a dog? Kids, sure. Property, cars, money, those made sense. He could even get on board with duking it out over membership to the country club. But a dog?

Must be one helluva cute mutt. He checked the address Jolene had sent to his phone. He was about three minutes away. He didn't need to consult the GPS since he knew Berkeley like the back of his hand.

Parking in a high-end neighborhood, he had to admit, he was impressed. He remembered Gregory Day. The guy was money. Big money, and an ass about it. The kind who made people come to him, not the other way around. Yet his wife dropped her fancy dog at a small, local groomer instead of some fancy dog salon? Why?

Heaving a sigh, Percy rolled out of his painstakingly re-stored '67 Corvette, pocketing his keys as his eyes swept from one side of the picket-fenced little house to the other.

Flowers spilled in a waterfall of melting pinks, purples and reds over and around the pale blue patio in a welcom-ing wave. A statue of a prancing dog stood next to the white door, one of the many canine figurines scattered through the postcard-size yard. Fitting, he supposed, since the small sign on the gate proclaimed this to be "Fur"sace Grooming.

"Fur"sace? Like Versace, the designer? Percy snickered. Cute.

Still, as pretentious as it sounded, someone clearly loved what they did. And he was about to make their job a whole lot harder. He glanced at his smartphone, noting that Jolene had uploaded the legal documents that said, yes indeed, one Chinese Crested by the name of Medusa had been awarded to Gregory Day. It should be enough to get the groomer to hand the dog over.

"One pup, coming up," he muttered as he checked the door. Finding it unlocked, he stepped inside. The entry was small and bright, trimmed in purple-and-pink stripes. But the un-natural quiet made the hair on the back of his neck stand on end. Shouldn't there be yipping mutts?

Passing through a tiny kitchen, he glanced into a large room that looked like a puppy playground. Pillows and toys and a mini trampoline took up one side of the room. A big-screen TV and a treadmill filled the other half. But no peo-ple. And no dogs.

Percy moved on.

At the other end of the hall, the lower half of a door was

shut. Through the open upper half he heard grumbles and rumbles. He moved closer, glancing carefully around the door frame.

Metal crates filled with a rainbow of fluffy blankets ranged the walls. Pampered pooches, indeed. Their beds looked cozier than his own.

And finally, he saw the dogs. There were at least a dozen of them, all curled up on their pillows. How'd the groomer get them all to sleep at the same time? That wasn't natural, was it? His spine tingled, warning Percy that a dramatic scene was the least of his worries. His quick and easy canine rescue was definitely going to be a big ole pain in the ass.

Percy reached beneath his light jacket to the small of his back and pulled out his gun. Sure, it was overkill, but he couldn't ignore the itchy feeling on the back of his neck.

Holding the weapon low, he surreptitiously rounded the last corner. Grooming room? He noted the sinks and tables, the scent of flowery shampoo and something else. Something sexy that gnawed at his memory, turning up the heat on his libido, even though he didn't know why.

"What the…"

A man in his line of work saw a lot of things. At thirty-two, he figured he was well past the age of being shocked.

But… Holy shit.

He didn't know what was the bigger kick to the gut. Seeing Andrea Tanner, the very woman who'd had top billing for three months straight in his most prurient sexual fantasies despite crushing his heart beneath her unknowing stiletto heel.

Or finding her, here, in an upscale canine beauty parlor. Tied to a chair. Her long, golden-brown curls were a mess and the green bandanna tied around her mouth made her hair mushroom around her in an angry halo. Brown eyes, so big and doelike with their lush fringe of lashes, widened in what looked like horror.

Percy's ego, once so strong and healthy, whimpered a little. Clearly, this little meeting was a surprise for both of them.

Then he saw the angry red marks on her arms where she'd struggled against the ropes that tied her to the chair. Fury surged, almost knocking him on his ass. Sure, he might have entertained the idea of tying Andrea up himself. But in his dreams, he'd had her permission, they were naked and they took turns. But this? He could see she wasn't hurt. Pissed, but not damaged. Still, whoever did this, he was kicking their ass.

Cocking his head, he did a finger swirl to indicate the room. Was there anyone still here? Andrea shook her head, no. Still, Percy did a quick scan of the room. He looked under tables, inside cabinets. Assured that they were alone, he holstered his gun.

Brow furrowed, he sauntered across the room. He shook his head at the slender figure staring at him through tear-drenched eyes. Even wet and filled with angry despair, her brown gaze was compelling. Lushly lashed, meltingly dark and hypnotically expressive.

Her hair gleamed, damp strands clinging to her flushed face and long, slender neck before cascading over her bare shoulders. The fantasy of that silky hair teasing the hot, slick hardness of his naked body had kept him awake many a night. Long after he'd given up hope of the fantasy ever being a reality.

"Okay, first things first," he said, pulling the bandanna out of her mouth. "Are you okay?"

"I'm okay. He's gone—"

Before she could say more, he tugged the bandanna back into place. Sure, he wanted to know who did this. It'd make kicking that person's ass easier. But first, he couldn't resist the gift in front of him. A chance to tell Andrea a few things while she was hog-tied and gagged. It was probably the only way he'd get her to listen to him.

"What a surprise," he said, offering his most charming smile. "If it isn't the luscious Andrea Tanner. Didn't we have a date? Did you forget? Or, what, you got tied up?"

That shifted the gleam in her eyes from tears to anger. Good. He'd rather deal with an angry woman than a weepy one any day. Especially one he had such strong feelings for.

Like a cork shooting out of a bottle, all his frustration, hurt and, yes, anger, suddenly spewed out.

"So what happened, Andrea? You had to hurry out to talk to a man about a dog? That's why you couldn't wake me up before you left? And, oh, I know. The dog ate your phone. That's why you didn't return my calls."

He acknowledged, if only to himself, that it was that last part that infuriated him the most. He'd never called a woman twice in his life. He'd never had to. Once they had his number, they ran after him.

"And now, after months of wondering what the hell happened, I walk in and find you tied up like a present. My very own present. What part shall I unwrap first, hmm?"

Despite his anger, Percy couldn't stop his gaze from traveling over the soft swell of her breasts emphasized by the damp cotton of her dress. Even rumpled and tear-stained, with the anger shooting off her in sparks, she was still gorgeous. Throw in clever, sweet and funny and there you had it.

She was the woman of his dreams. And she wanted nothing to do with him.

PERCY GRAHAM? PERCY FREAKING Graham? She'd been threatened, yelled at, then bound and gagged by a man who had a serious disdain for deodorant. She was tied to a chair and dripping in sweat because some huge smelly goon had fallen against her thermostat and busted it, terrified of one tiny dog. Most of all, she was worried sick about the precious puppies entrusted to her care.

And now Percy Graham walks in?

Were the gods punishing her for something?

Andrea Tanner was a good woman. She paid her bills on time, was kind to the deranged and lavished love and attention on animals and children. Her mother, who was admittedly biased, claimed her to be beautiful despite the extra fifteen pounds she insisted Andrea needed to lose. Her clients loved her and the neighborhood ladies' club had recently voted her Best New Business.

So, dammit, why was her life taking a spin cycle through hell and bringing with it the one man she never wanted to see again?

Karmic payback. Clearly, every terror she had was visiting today. Smelly goons, being tied up and helpless, the sexiest man on earth. Her eyes shot from one corner of the room to another. Giant spiders had to be next.

"What are you doing here?" she tried to ask Percy. But the rag was still in her mouth, so her words came out a muffled grumble.

"You know, I've entertained quite a few fantasies about you," Percy said as he rocked back on the heels of his worn boots. That wicked curve of his lips engaged his sneakiest weapon. The man's dimple. Andrea swore she could feel her girlie parts start melting right through her stress, anger and embarrassment. Him, the most gorgeous man on earth, having fantasies about her? Oh, baby. "But even in my imagination, I never thought you'd go for the bondage thing. Maybe I should grab a bottle of wine and see where this goes?"

Andrea's gag-muffled growl only made him laugh. Even though she knew it was futile, she strained and struggled against her bindings. She had no clue what she'd do if she got free. Run after the guy who stole her dog? Shake her fists at the heavens? Or more likely, give in to the deep-seated urge she always had whenever she was around Percy. To clamp her thighs around his waist and beg for a ride.

Willing to risk the humiliation of throwing herself at a man with his own happy harem, she growled her demand that he free her. Whether he was used to gagged orders or just intuitive enough to figure out what she'd said, Percy stepped closer. His scent, rich and masculine with a welcome whiff of clean, enveloped her as he reached behind her head to work at the knotted fabric.

His fingers tangled in her hair. Her heart jumped as those same fingers gently smoothed the damp tresses away from the rag. Her breath caught in her chest as she stared at his chest, the sprinkling of dark hair visible through his open collar. It

s right there, close enough to bury her nose in. Or if he'd
rry up and get the gag off her mouth.

Thankfully, as soon as he got the fabric unknotted, he
pped back. She should demand he untie her, too. But she
uld only take so much. Having a few minutes to recover be-
e he came within nibbling distance again was a good thing.

"How'd you know I needed help?" she asked instead, work-
g her jaw to try to ease the tension.

"I didn't. I'm here to pick up a dog." Looming over her, the
rn denim fabric of his crotch level with her face a constant
traction, he added, "What're you doing here?"

"This is my puppy salon." Pride sang in her words as she
lowed his gaze. "Fur"sace was all hers.

"You do dogs' hair?" He gave her a frown, his eyes travel-
g over her body in a way that made her tingle with desire.
s blue eyes warmed and that wicked smile played at the
rner of his lips as if he knew exactly how hot he made her
th just one look. "Aren't you a woman of many talents."

Wasn't she just. There was one particular talent she had
t involved an ice cube, a feather and two scarves.

No. Even with those talents, she still couldn't handle a
manizer like Percy Graham. All it'd taken were a couple
dates for her to realize that she was way out of her league
th a guy like him. But she'd figured, hey, why not enjoy tip-
ing through the stars while she had a chance? Then she'd
de the biggest mistake of her life. She'd slept with him.

She'd always figured sex was supposed to make her feel
od.

But sex with a guy like Percy? A man with the face of an
gel and the body of a Greek god? Sex with him had made
r feel amazing.

And it'd scared the living bejeezus out of her.

Because there was no way an average girl like her could

keep a guy like Percy. She'd woken up, naked in his ar
as the sun was rising, and had freaked. There she was, ca
ing around an extra fifteen pounds, too self-conscious to
the deed with the lights on—let alone do anything clever
kinky—and beset by so many issues she might as well
chained to a giant boulder.

She'd done what any smart, independent woman wou
do. She'd sneaked out of his bed and run as fast as she cou

And now, lookie lookie, here he was. Just what she need

But, wait… He was just what she needed. Percy was a
One with tracking devices and cool equipment and possil
satellite-spy stuff. Her breath caught in her chest.

"Someone kidnapped one of my dogs," she finally sa
terror for the poor thing surfacing again, overriding bo
her shock at seeing Percy and the intense spike in sex
awareness that was making her thighs melt. "I have to
her back. I have to rescue her. You're here. You can help
I can pay you."

His eyes sharpened. He looked pissed for a second, as
the idea of her offering him money was an insult. Then
shrugged it off.

"Sorry. I'm in a hurry," he dismissed as he poked into
dog crate on the table before bending down to look bene
it. "I'll untie you, finish my business and then I've got a pla
to catch. You tell me who did this and I'll kick their ass
my way to the airport."

She got all giddy for a second at the idea of him avengi
her honor. Then she realized it was just a knee-jerk reacti
for a guy like Percy. Three good deeds required before di
ner, or no dessert.

"I've got an emergency here," she snapped. "Someo
stole a dog. They tied me to this chair. And all you're w
ried about is catching a plane?"

"Relax. Nobody's gonna hurt some cute little dog."

How could he be so dismissive? Andrea glared. She'd hardly call Mr. Testosterone naive, but she knew perfectly well that there were plenty of people who didn't think twice about hurting animals—cute and little or not. Eliza, Medusa's owner, had regaled Andrea with stories about how horrible her soon-to-be ex-husband was to poor little Snookie Bumpkins, as she insisted on calling the dog.

Because while Medusa was definitely little at eight pounds, she was anything but cute. Or sweet. Actually, she was one of the snottiest dogs Andrea had ever worked with. Something the dognapper had been bitching about when he'd shoved the tiny Chinese Crested into a carrier.

Which only added to poor Medusa's danger.

"I have to get Medusa back," Andrea said, almost in tears as she tugged at the ropes binding her. "Untie me, please. I've got to go."

Percy barely moved, but she swore he came to full attention. His gaze skewered her, a frown creasing his brow as he walked back over to her.

"You said the dog's name is Medusa?" He waited for her nod before he knelt down to untie her foot from the chair leg. Andrea forced herself not to lean forward—just three inches—and bury her face in his hair, seeking comfort. "Owner's Gregory Day?"

"No. That bully has no claim on the dog," she said absently as she stretched her now-free left leg out and rotated her ankle. "The owner is Eliza Conner-Day."

"Same diff," he retorted as he went to work freeing her other leg. It was all she could do to keep her fingers from burying themselves in his thick golden-brown hair. "That's the dog I was hired to pick up. Give me the deets and I'll track it down."

Fear and defiance duked it out in Andrea's stomach. Fear for that poor little dog pushed her to agree. The sooner some one who knew what they were doing found her, the better.

But Medusa was still technically in her care. And she'd already lost one dog this year—a sneaky little bulldog had tunneled out while Andrea had been busy breaking up a potentially horrific date between a shepherd and a dachshund. She'd found the dog that same evening, eating carrots out of the neighboring community garden. But still, if word got out that she'd lost another dog, her business could be ruined.

And that meant she couldn't let Percy—or anyone who'd report this back to Eliza, like the police—take over. No. She had to get the dog back herself. Or, she narrowed her eyes at Percy, with a little help.

"I'm going with you," she decided, getting to her feet and shaking the stiffness out of her limbs. "I'll pay you for your time and we'll rescue the dog together."

"I don't think so."

"No me, no deets," she said with a stubborn tilt of her chin.

She was getting that dog back. Even if she had to spend time with the sexiest man in the world to do it.

She could almost hear her battered ego whimpering out a warning. But not even Percy Graham could break her heart and destroy her self-worth on a dog-rescue mission.

Could he?

3

PERCY KNEW HE SHOULD WALK AWAY. A quick glance at his watch said there were only six hours left before his flight. Leaving was smart. He could call from the car, forward the case to Matthews and call it a partnership test. If he left now, he'd have plenty of time to finish packing and get to the airport early enough to avoid the worst of the TSA gropes.

And more important, he'd avoid any further exposure to the woman who'd rejected him. If he stuck around, who knew what could happen? Hell, he might start spouting poetry or making crazy promises.

Yep. Time to go.

Halfway to the door, his gaze landed on Andrea. She was flitting to and fro, gathering things for her canine rescue mission. She looked so earnest. And, dammit, so worried.

Why was she so damn gorgeous? Even sweaty, out of breath and muttering to herself, she made his mouth water. Long strands of brown hair curled around a face that made him think crazy thoughts. Made him want to beg her to give them a chance. But he'd never begged in his life and he wasn't about to start now. A man had his pride, after all. A woman slept with a guy, then refused to take his calls or see him again? That didn't make for a promising fresh start. He wasn't sure his fragile ego could take another direct hit.

Like a magnet to steel, his gaze followed her as she bent over a low cabinet, the purple cotton of her dress molding across the sweet curve of her butt as she leaned down. His mouth watered. His body hardened. He'd spent the last three months distracted by her memory. Dreaming of reveling in the heaven of her body, only to be denied ever visiting again when she'd didn't return his calls.

He was sure that distraction was part of his failure problem. If he could get over it, he'd regain his savvy, brilliant investigative talents, his mental balance and his damn sense of humor.

Maybe what he needed more than a vacation was a chance to get over Andrea.

And she needed him.

That just might give him the edge.

What he was going to do with that edge, he wasn't sure. His ego said payback. His body said pleasure. His eyes landed on the ropes curled, snakelike, around the chair legs. His instincts screamed at him to protect her and solve this case.

And the wise part of his brain warned that sticking around, spending time with Andrea, meant risk. To his pride, at the least. His heart, at the most.

The problem with wisdom was it was so easy to ignore.

"So," he started to say. He stopped to clear the husky desire from his throat, then tried again. "So, can you tell me what happened here today?"

"What happened was a big stinky jerk broke in, stole a dog that I was entrusted to care for and tied me up. Thankfully, though, you showed up. You can help me get her back."

"I was hired to pick the dog up here, not to go chasing after it," Percy countered. Not that there was any question that he'd be giving chase. But he planned to do it alone.

"Fine. Then I'll hire you to help me get the dog back so you can do your other job." Her smile was pure sass. Damned if he didn't find that totally sexy.

Before he could tell her no, or better yet, hell, no, she ran from the room. Knowing he had no choice, Percy followed her into the room filled with luxuriously kenneled sleeping dogs.

She rushed from cage to cage, checking the dogs. She lifted eyelids. She checked pulses. In the case of a big, fat-headed Rottweiler, she opened the cage and pressed kisses on its brow. The dog gave a huge snorting sort of snore in response.

Then Andrea burst into tears. Horrified, Percy almost turned tail and scurried from the room. Women in tears scared him more than staring down a loaded gun barrel.

"Are you okay?" he forced himself to ask, cringing.

"He promised he wouldn't hurt them. He said he put a small dose of something in their food to make them sleep so they'd stay quiet. But I wasn't sure. I was so afraid…"

He couldn't help it. Even as his emotional survival instincts screamed warning, Percy stepped forward to take her into his arms. His heart sighed, even as he steeled himself against letting her get to him.

She obviously wasn't worried about his reaction. She sobbed, soaking his shirt. She gulped, making him worry she might hyperventilate. And she did absolutely nothing provocative or sensual to turn him on.

But the spiced floral fragrance of her hair filled his senses. The way her fingers gripped his shirt, kneading and working the fabric against the hard flesh of his chest, went straight to his head, filling it with images of her gripping his back in the same way while he'd plunged into the welcoming depths of her body.

Percy's head swam and his breath caught in his throat as she shifted, burrowing deeper in his arms. Trying to focus on offering comfort instead of offering his body, he rubbed his hands over the soft flesh of her shoulders. It was like sliding his fingers over silk. God, she felt good. As she sobbed, she curved her lush figure tighter against his rapidly hardening erection.

She was pure temptation. He'd already been tempted once, though. And he'd come away with his first-ever broken heart. A smart man would have turned and run at the first sniffle. Yet here he was, hanging on to Andrea as if she was the answer to his every prayer and reveling in the fact that she'd turned to him for comfort.

Yeah, he told himself, wincing and shifting his hips away from temptation. Crying women were scary as hell.

"C'mon," he said, trying to sound stern. He stopped caressing and gripped her shoulders, shifting her to a semisafe distance away from his body. "Crying isn't going to help anything."

"I was so worried, though," she said with a sniff as she scrubbed her hands over her cheeks. "I love these dogs as if they were my own. That rottie there, Tinkerbell? She is my own. And he drugged them. That nasty man tied me up and drugged my dogs. I could just kill him," she added with emphasis.

"He left you here, tied up like that, unable to take care of the dogs, all weekend?" Why that made him even angrier, Percy didn't know.

"It wouldn't have been weekend. I mean, Dina, my assistant, she's due in ten minutes. But he didn't know that," she said after glancing at the wall clock. "I need to call the vet and have him meet her here. The dogs all need to be checked."

"Good. You do that. I'll go get that other dog back and deal with the creep."

She blinked a couple of times and took a deep breath. The glistening tears in her eyes were replaced by a wary distrust.

What the hell?

What had he done to earn that reaction?

Before he could ask, she spun out of his arms and hurried out of the room. Unable to help himself, he followed in time to see her grab a huge bag covered in glitter, with the name Medusa inscribed in rhinestones.

"Do you have any idea who this guy was?" Percy asked. "Why'd he take the dog? Do you think he was hired muscle, or was he acting alone?"

Andrea frowned, a fluffy blanket in one hand and what looked like a bunch of tiny diapers in the other. "What difference does it make if he was being paid or not?"

"Motivation will help us find the dog," Percy said.

A tiny furrow wrinkling her brow, Andrea paused in the act of adding to the bag what looked like an oversize knitted sock with the toes cut out and a feathered fringe. "But I know where the dog is. So motivation doesn't matter. We just have to get her."

"Motivation always matters." Then he sighed. "But I can deal with that later. Tell me where she is."

"I'll tell you how to get there when we're on our way."

"What do you mean, on our way?" Horror overshadowed desire. "You're not going with me."

No way. He had a job to do. A dognapper's ass to kick for tying up Andrea and making her cry. And he had a plane to catch for a vacation that he needed even more desperately now than he had this morning.

"Tell me what you know," he cajoled with a smile that had never failed to charm. "I'll get the dog, punch that guy out for you, and when I turn the dog over to Day, I'll make sure he knows what you went through."

There. All the bases covered. He waited for her agreement, and hopefully one of those incredible smiles. And since he was a man who believed in tempting fate, maybe even a sweetly grateful kiss of thanks before he left.

As Percy smiled that warm, heart-melting smile of his, Andrea almost nodded. Then she stopped and frowned. Did anyone ever say no to him?

It wasn't just the fact that he was gorgeous that made him dangerous, although he was. It was that he was sweet, charming, smart and so damn good at everything. Everything. He had women throwing themselves at his feet, all desperate to be the one who didn't say no.

A part of her—a teensy, ignorable part—wondered if that's why she'd run from Percy without explanation. Because she'd been desperate to stand out from his crowd of adoring admirers. Beautiful, sexy, skinny admirers.

Maybe it was so easy to ignore that teensy part because she knew perfectly well she already stood out from all those women. She wasn't beautiful, she wasn't sexy. And no amount of dieting seemed to make a dent in the extra fifteen pounds padding her curves, so her mother's assurance that she had such a pretty face wasn't much consolation.

Despite Percy's gorgeous smile and sweetly worded request, she was going to have to say no to him one more time.

"I'm sorry, but I can't agree to that," she told him. "If I tell you how to find Medusa, you'll leave me behind. She's not the most trusting dog under the best of circumstances and she's particularly fragile right now. She knows me. She trusts me. So I'm going."

"You don't think I can handle a little dog?" His laugh was

pure masculine confidence. Andrea wondered what it was like to be that self-assured.

"Nobody can handle Medusa," Andrea told him, laughing at the idea as she finished gathering the dog's necessities. Sable brush. Organic doggie treats. La Mer moisturizing cream. "She is a very rare, extremely expensive dog. She's used to being treated a certain way and has a distinctive personality."

"In other words, she's a spoiled brat of a dog?"

Andrea wrinkled her nose, but didn't disagree. "As for the rest, it doesn't matter how you spin it. If you rescue Medusa without me and return her to my client's soon-to-be ex-husband, my business will be ruined. Diamonds and Doggies will make sure of it."

She'd have insisted on going out of worry for Medusa. But just thinking about her rival groomer only amped up her resolve.

"What is Diamonds and Doggies?"

"It's a high-end dog-grooming boutique. The owner, Raye Jensen, claims there's room for only one groomer to the elite in the Bay Area. When I opened my salon, she warned me to stay out of her way. If she gets word that a dog in my care was stolen, and then handed over to that miserable excuse for an ex-owner, Day, she'll have all the ammunition she's been looking for to steal every one of my clients."

Andrea had finished packing while she was talking. Digging into her purse, she found her keys and used one to open the glass-fronted cabinet. Her fingers closed on the small metal wand at the same time she heard the bells over the front door jangle. She grabbed the device and tossed it into her purse, then pulled the dog's tote bag over her shoulder and turned to Percy.

"All set," she told him. "Just give me a second to fill Dina in and call the vet."

He was busy making notes.

"What're you doing?"

"Adding your rival groomer to my list of people with motivation to steal a dog." He pocketed the notepad and gave her a long look before shaking his head. "I'd really rather you stay here. If this dog is as expensive as you say, they might call with a ransom demand or something."

"I'm going," she insisted. "You can't find her without me, so there's no point in arguing."

He gave her a look that was a mixture of frustration, calculation and impatience.

But underneath she saw desire. Intense, sexual heat with the promise of soul-stirring satisfaction.

A promise she knew he could keep.

Andrea gulped.

That, right there, was why she'd run away from him three months ago. Because the minute he gave her that look—like he wanted to nibble chocolate off her toes—she lost her senses. And given that he was the most sexual man she'd ever met, with women throwing themselves at him left and right, she knew there was no way he'd be interested long-term in her pudgy, unremarkable self.

"Setting aside the fact that I work alone," he said quietly, his voice low and tempting, "do you think it's a good idea for the two of us to spend so much time together? I mean, you obviously had a reason to put an end to us before. Are you prepared to explain that? And to take a chance on whatever's going to happen when I've got you all to myself for a few hours?"

Tiny shivers spun through her system as Andrea tried to catch her breath. The images of the two of them wrapped

round each other in the dark flashed in delicious Technicolor.
he knew she didn't want to explain herself. If she'd been
ble to do that, she would have that morning, instead of run-
ing away.

But what might happen in the few hours they'd be together?

That, she wasn't so sure she wanted to avoid.

Still, it was a risk she had to take if she wanted to save
he dog and her reputation. The only question was, could her
eart hold out?

4

As HE WAITED—NOT SO PATIENTLY—in his car for Andrea t
do whatever she had to do with her assistant, Percy barel
refrained from pounding his forehead on the steering whee
His mother had always warned him to be careful what h
wished for. And this was a perfect example. He finally g
what he'd spent the last three months wishing for. Andre
Tanner, begging for his company.

And it wasn't because of his hot body or his incredible kiss
ing style. Nor for his looks and his great personality. Nop
it was over some damn dog.

This was stupid. He should go. He could tell Day he'
handed off the case, let the cops take over and get himsel
on that plane. Away from temptation.

Before he could do the smart thing and leave, Andrea ra
out the door, her long hair flying behind her as she hurried t
join him. She had a purse over one shoulder, that flashy tot
bag over the other and a worried frown on her face. As sh
leaned into the car to toss the tote behind the seat, the brigl
purple fabric of her dress pulled tight against her lush bod
His mouth watered.

Nope. As tempting as she was, he wasn't going to go dow

hat path. Not again. They'd get the dog, solve the case. He could chalk this up to paying karma back with change, and get back to his happily charmed life.

"You said you know where the dog is, right? So where to?" he asked. Once she told him, he could escort her right back out of the car and out of temptation's reach.

"Head toward San Francisco," she hedged.

Percy shot her a look, noting the suspicious set of her chin. Smart girl. Fine.

Telling himself to at least pretend to be irritated to have to spend more time with her, he frowned.

"Tell me why someone would kidnap this dog." He pulled away from the curb as soon as she hooked her seat belt. "Do you think it has anything to do with the custody battle? I saw the paperwork. My client got the dog and his ex got a house, so money plays in. But why the drama? What's the motivation for dognapping?"

Andrea pursed her lips, their glossy fullness making his mouth water. Even though he knew he should be trying to get rid of her, another part of him—the part that thought sex was the answer to everything—figured having her around might not be all bad. Maybe now he could get her out of his system.

"Medusa is a rare Chinese Crested. Her pedigree is stellar. In fact, her sire was commanding five-figure stud fees. She's the last of his line, which makes her value even higher."

"So money is the most obvious motivator."

"Sure, I suppose it could be. She's worth a bundle. But only if she's claimed publicly. To command that kind of money, the dog's pedigree has to be documented and shared. You can't breed a dog and pretend it's another one."

As she was talking, Andrea shifted in her seat. Drawing one knee up so the bright purple fabric of her dress slipped into temptingly dangerous territory, she curled her hand

around her ankle and tilted her head back, then side to side
as if stretching out the tension.

"Hmm," was all Percy could offer, since his tongue, among
other things, was swollen.

Turning onto University Avenue, he was glad traffic de
manded his attention. Only his worry about damaging his pre
cious Vette seemed strong enough to keep him from leaning
over to lick his way up the silky-smooth skin of Andrea's leg
until he discovered what color her panties were.

To distract himself, he punched a key on his cell phone so
it rang through the Bluetooth strategically hidden in his car's
dash. Five rings later and the canned message telling him his
offices were closed for the week came on.

"Dammit," he muttered, hanging up. He checked his watch
and growled. Jolene should have still been there.

"Did you think you were going to answer your own
phone?" Andrea teased with a laugh.

"I wanted my secretary to run some reports on the Days
Financials, custody dispute, divorce settlement. That kind
of thing."

For all its high dollar value, he was sure the dog's kidnap
ping had something to do with one, the other, or both of them

"Secretary, hmm?" Andrea's feet both dropped to the floor
and she shifted just a little toward the door, taking her sweet
scent farther away from him. Despite the warm June sun
shine, a light chill filled the car. "Let me guess. She's blonde
built and totally devoted to you?"

Bottle blond with iron-gray roots, built like a rusty steam
ship and totally devoted to bossing him around, maybe.

"Sure. Why not," he decided with a laugh. "And better yet
she knows how to keep me in line."

"The two of you must be ever so happy together," Andrea
said stiffly. Then, as if unable to help herself, she gave him a

narrow look. "Doesn't having her in the office interfere with your wild dating life?"

"I don't date people who work for me." Especially not people old enough to be his grandmother. "Don't tell me you're jealous. After all, you're the one who dumped me. Not the other way around, sweetheart."

Reminded of that little tidbit, Percy's smile fell away. Why had she blown him off? There was clearly heat between them. He was a good guy. He knew how to treat a lady and didn't skimp on dates. So what had gone wrong?

He figured it was a testament to how tired and burned out he was that the words almost slipped off his tongue. What a way to destroy what was left of his ego.

To distract himself from another close slipup, he focused on the case again.

"Day knew where the dog was today. How? Given the acrimonious state of their pending divorce, I can't see his ex-wife keeping him up-to-date with her schedule."

"Eliza is more than happy to share the nasty details of her divorce with anyone who will listen," Andrea said, relaxing again now that the topic was back on the dog. "She claims that she got custody of Medusa, while her husband got the house in Monterey. She can't be behind the dognapping."

Percy just shrugged. He had legal docs—and he'd have Jolene check them closer—that stated the dog belonged to Day.

"Sure, she could be," he told Andrea. "She knows her ex wants the dog. What better way to have your cake and eat it, too, than to arrange for it to be stolen. She creates some drama, pisses off her ex and hides the dog away until the settlement is done. Then, voila, suddenly she has a new dog."

Andrea was shaking her head before he finished talking. "She can't claim Medusa to be anything but herself."

"Why not? A dog's a dog."

"I told you before. Medusa's worth a fortune, but only if she's documented. So as soon as someone tries to show her or sell her puppies, they'd be outed. Eliza doesn't want her because she's a beloved pet. She wants her because she's a rare pedigree that's fun to show off. Kinda like the five-carat diamond she still wears despite the divorce."

"Classy."

Andrea chuckled. "Oh, yeah. Added to all of that, Medusa is due to come into heat any day now. That's why she was in the boutique, getting all prettied up for her, um, date."

Percy slid Andrea a sideways look and cringed. "Does that mean what I think it means?"

Andrea's laughter filled the car. The sound was pure joy, uninhibited and full of delight. It was all Percy could do not to pull over, drag her across the console and kiss her until she was as crazy with wanting as he was.

"Despite the pampering bath, hair and nail treatment and doggy facial, poor Medusa's date isn't pure romance. To prevent any possible damage by an, um, enthusiastic partner, the date will take place in a laboratory on Monday morning," she said, her words stiff and heavy.

"You sound upset."

Andrea sighed, her shoulders drooping before she gave a helpless shrug. "I don't have any right to be. I mean, she's a valuable commodity and her puppies will be worth a small fortune. And this kind of thing is pretty standard once you start dealing with dogs at this level."

Yeah. She was upset. Without thinking, Percy reached over and took her hand to give it a comforting squeeze. Her fingers curled into his, making him feel like a giddy schoolboy. Where the hell was his legendary cool with women now? Still, he was thrilled when she didn't pull away.

"That's why it can't be Eliza." Andrea gave a decisive nod. "It has to be Day. It'd be just like him to stage this elaborate drama to keep Medusa from her date."

"Hmm." Maybe. Or maybe not. His number-one rule in solving cases was to keep an open mind. "First things first. We rescue the dog. Then we figure out who's behind the dognapping."

He shot her a glance, wishing she'd stop nibbling on her lower lip. Or, if he was going to throw around wishes, maybe she could nibble on his instead.

"So where's the dog, exactly?" The sooner they got it, the sooner he could put some distance between himself and the misery of knowing Andrea didn't want him the way he wanted her. He'd never had to chase a woman in his life, and he wasn't about to start now. Not when the chase would clearly end with him empty-handed. Again.

IT WAS AS IF SOMEONE, somewhere, had peeked into Andrea's wildest dreams and brought Percy back into her life as the ultimate temptation. A larger-than-life hero swooping in to rescue her. All she could think of were the ways she wanted to thank him.

Most of them started with her undressing him with her teeth, and ended with her begging him to let her be a part of his life. Her fingers still clinging to the warm strength of his, Andrea sighed. Because while she might have a lousy dating record, enough extra weight on her to make bathing-suit season a misery and a little bit of trouble standing up for herself…she wasn't a masochist.

"Andrea?" Percy prompted. "Where's the dog? How do you know how to find it?"

Focus on the task at hand, she lectured herself. Again. Let Percy work his magic to find the dog and save her career.

"As I mentioned, Medusa is really valuable," she said, giving her fingers a tug, trying to free them from his grip.

When he wouldn't let go, she sighed and moved their hands toward the console instead of being so temptingly close to her heat. After the day she'd had, who knew what crazy things she might do in a moment of stress-induced comfort seeking. Like take his hand and slide it right up her skirt.

"So?"

"So, like most dogs who are either well-loved or worth a lot, she's been microchipped. And she's wearing a GPS tracker."

"Huh?" He looked over, questions in his eyes clear even through his sunglasses. "She's trackable? Did you call whoever she's registered with?"

Andrea gave the tiniest of winces. She hated admitting things like this. It wasn't that it was wrong to have a GPS tracking device. That was just smart business. What was wrong was that she didn't tell her clients that as soon as the dog was left in her care, she put a tracking device on their collar. Just in case. She'd been determined to never lose another one, even briefly. So much for that resolution.

"I've got the GPS monitor to track her," she admitted. Tugging her hand free, she grabbed the device out of her bag and held it up. There on the screen was a red beeping light next to a San Francisco address.

"That's awesome. You're so damn clever." He shot her a smile that made desire curl tight in her belly. Andrea's heart bumped a little faster and she swallowed, suddenly wondering if this whole thing was some kind of gift from the gods. A hint for her to give Percy a chance. To get past her fear of not measuring up to all his other women.

Then he glanced at his watch. "We can grab the mutt, drop you back at your place. We'll call the happy ex-couple and have them both meet us there so you can hash this out. And I'll still have plenty of time to catch my flight."

The desire in her belly fizzled like a wet firecracker. That's right. He was on his way to a decadent beach vacation. For all she knew, he had a girlfriend going, too. Or he'd find a woman there. More likely, one would find him. They'd only gone on four dates before she'd given in to the intense sexual tension and gone to bed with him. Every single date had included another woman. Sometimes more than one. Hitting on him, as if she were invisible. Reminding him of where they'd met, or dated or slept together. It'd been too much for Andrea to take. When she'd woken in his arms to the sound of a husky voice on his answering machine, offering to bring him some morning delight, she'd realized she just couldn't handle the pressure. So she'd run.

And he hadn't run after her.

"Take Seventh Street," she said with a sigh, trying to accept that the only reason fate had brought him back into her life was to save the dog. Not to make all her dreams—sexual and otherwise—come true.

Twenty minutes later, Percy parked on a steep hill. The two of them glanced at the GPS screen, then at the high-rise apartment building across the street.

"She's in there?" he asked.

"According to this, she is."

But where? There had to be hundreds of apartments in that building. She looked helplessly at Percy, glad he and his expertise were here. If not, she knew she'd be wandering the hallways, GPS in hand like a metal detector mining for doggie gold.

One hand on the door to exit, she hesitated. Swallowing hard, she turned back to face him.

"Are you going in there to get the dog for your client?" she asked quietly. "Or to give her back to me?"

Dark lenses hid his intense blue eyes but she could still feel his stare. After a few seconds, he took off his sunglasses and slowly tilted his head toward the building.

"If you want me to do this job for you instead of Day, you have to pay the price."

Her stomach sank.

"I can't afford to match whatever Day's paying you."

The look he gave her was hot enough to melt her dress right off. Andrea's breath lodged in a tight ball in her throat, making swallowing impossible.

"I'm not talking money, sweetheart."

5

OH, BABY. ANDREA WAS AFRAID she was going to drool. What price did he mean? Could he mean what she thought he meant? Before she could figure out how to ask without sounding like an idiot if she was wrong, he got out of the car.

Well. She frowned. So much for that.

Deflated, she tossed the GPS into her purse and slung it over her shoulder, then opened the passenger door. And there was Percy.

Taking her hand, he pulled her from the car.

"What's the—"

Before she could complete her nervous question, his mouth took hers. Hot. Intense. Wild.

Oh, baby.

It was as good as she remembered. The taste of him, rich and tempting on her tongue. The scent of him, wrapping around her like a hug. The feel of his hard body against her softer curves.

His tongue swept over her mouth, making her want to whimper in delight. She was a heartbeat away from parting her lips to invite him in when he pulled back.

He looked calm enough, but she could see the edgy heat

in his eyes. Could feel the pounding of his heart against her breast. And, gratifyingly, the delicious pressure of his growing hard-on against her thigh.

"What was that?" she said, trying to sound shocked and offended. It was a bummer that her low, husky tone came across as one hundred percent hot and horny instead.

"That, sweetheart, was the down payment on my fee."

"You don't really think I'm going to, what? Sleep with you in exchange for services rendered? Don't you have a little more respect for both of us than that?" Pretending she wasn't tempted, Andrea gave him a chiding look as she reluctantly peeled her body off his.

"I have complete respect," he said, releasing her so slowly she wasn't sure he was going to let go. "I also have a lot of respect for tying up loose ends. You and me, sweetheart? We've got some loose ends to take care of before we say goodbye this time."

Terror tangled with desire in a hot, tight knot low in Andrea's belly. She didn't know what to say. She didn't even know what to think. Her body was still humming, urging her to straddle his waist and agree to anything.

Trying to clear her head, she hurried around him. Her shoe caught on the curb, almost sending her sprawling. Percy came to the rescue, leaping forward and grabbing her before she could tumble backward. He pulled her tight against his body, his arm wrapped around her shoulders as if to keep her from bolting. But she didn't want to move away. Nope, she'd rather stay here, curled against the muscular length of him. Or better yet, to strip him naked and kiss her way down his body right here on a public street.

This powerful pull of hot attraction, the desperate need to be with Percy, was overwhelming. But the speculation in his eyes, combined with that sexy smile, was all the warning she needed to remember all the reasons he should be off-limits. But he was right about the loose ends. She'd walked away from him once already, but she hadn't been able to get him out of her mind. Maybe this time, with a real, official goodbye, her heart—and her body—would accept that it was over.

Swallowing hard to get past the aching desire to grab him for one more taste to assure herself that she was making the right decision, Andrea pulled away.

"Fine," she blurted. She'd hate herself if she turned him down. She was afraid she'd hate herself for saying yes. Since she was going to having a hatefest either way, she might as well enjoy herself. And, more important, she'd get him out of her system in a way that offered closure instead of daily regrets. "You work for me from now on instead of Day. And I'll pay your price."

WELL, HELL. LOOK WHAT HAPPENED. He let lust overrule his brain. He deserved a swift kick in the ass. Andrea was the kind of woman who deserved poetry. Moonlight and flowers and sweet words of devotion. Not a skeezy sex-for-hire deal. He'd been about to tell her that he was teasing, that he wasn't going to turn the dog over to Day until he figured out who was behind the dognapping. But then she'd done the unthinkable.

She'd accepted his proposition.

His ego limped into the corner to pout. For himself, she'd sneaked out at daybreak and pretended he didn't exist. Now she was willing to sleep with him again, but only to save a dog?

This must be someone's way of punishing him for previous misdeeds. Because he knew he should tell her he wasn't going to accept sex for his services. That he'd help her for nothing. But Andrea tasted so delicious. Her lips were pure ambrosia, her body a delight from heaven. So his vocal cords froze on the words.

Get the dog first, he decided. Then he'd tell her he'd been kidding.

"Let's go," he said, taking her arm to guide her across the street toward the apartment building. As they crossed, he considered and discarded their various options. The simplest way was best. "We'll hit each floor with the tracking device until it lights up strong enough to indicate the dog is there. When we find the apartment, you stay back. Hide around a corner or something, while I talk to the guy."

"You're just going to, what? Talk him into handing over Medusa?"

Percy grinned. The skepticism in her tone made it clear that Andrea wasn't impressed with her choice to hire him.

"I'm going to case the place. See where the dog is, check outside accessibility. I want to make sure there's a window or outside door. Once I've got a visual, we'll distract the guy while I sneak in and grab the dog."

"Distract the guy? With what? A donut?"

"Hey, good idea. I was going to have a pizza delivered, but donuts will work, too."

He reached for the handle to the apartment complex's entrance and gave her a questioning look.

"Ready?" he asked.

"Ready," she agreed, her smile flashing bright. Bright enough to almost hide the edge of nerves he saw lurking in her eyes and in the way her fingers twisted her purse strap. Given that she'd already come out on the wrong end of one encounter with this guy today, Percy couldn't blame her.

Giving in to the urgings of the devilish voice in his head, he slid one hand over the curve of her cheek and tilted her head up to meet his lips. Her gasp ended in a fluttering sigh as he paid gentle homage to her mouth. She leaned into him, her body soft and sweet. It was all he could do not to dive deeper, to take the kiss from tender to torrid with a thrust of his tongue. But they were on a mission. So he kept his tongue to himself and slowly pulled away to give her a reassuring smile.

"It's gonna be fine," he promised.

Andrea gazed into Percy's eyes and gave a deep sigh. Oh, yeah. Everything was going to be just fine. Despite the nerves still jumping beneath the desire in her belly, she had total faith that he'd rescue Medusa and save her business. And that paying him for his assistance was going to be one of the sweetest, most emotionally expensive bills of her life.

"Hey, you're blocking the door."

Andrea jumped back, making room for the elderly woman with her standard poodle. The dog pranced, a red bow high on her black curls. The woman stomped past, a purple backpack matching her tightly curled hair.

Grinning, Andrea met Percy's laughing eyes. Her heart melted a little, both at their shared humor and at how sweet he looked holding the door open for the lady and her dog.

"Thanks. Gotta get Duke here to the dog yard before he embarrasses us," the woman muttered.

Duke? Percy mouthed.

Andrea barely stifled her laugh. She watched the prancing and stomping pair make their way across the lobby to an atrium door marked Pets: Tenants Only. Through the heavy glass, she saw a doggie paradise. Grass, play structures, benches for the owners to relax and a huge water fountain.

"Wow. Most apartment buildings barely tolerate pets," she commented as she followed Percy into the lobby. "But this place makes them welcome. That's so great."

Just as the elevator door opened, she glanced out the window again. She gasped as her stomach dived into her toes.

"There she is!"

Without another word, not even looking to see if Percy was following, Andrea ran across the lobby. Her eyes never left the prancing dog who was playing queen of the bushes, running to and fro with three dogs chasing her.

"Oh, my…" Andrea almost screamed. Medusa was running free. With male dogs? Now? Just as her fingers closed over the door handle, Percy grabbed her around the waist and swung her away from the door.

"He's out there," he told her, not even winded after his sprint. "Let's be smart about this, okay? We want the dog, not a fight."

"I don't care about him," she argued, struggling to free herself from the hard strength of his arms. "I've got to get her. She's running loose. With male dogs. Oh, my God, this is a disaster."

"Calm down."

It was his tone, more than his command, that finally pierced the panic wrapping around Andrea. With a shuddering sigh, she quit thrashing and sank her body into his, grateful for the support.

"I don't want a fight," she agreed. "But we have to get her. Now. Before one of those dogs gets too friendly."

"Shit," he muttered, sounding embarrassed.

"We have to," she insisted. "Now."

"I know. I know. Just give me a second to plan it out."

Peeling her cheek off his chest, Andrea glanced up at Percy's face. He assessed the patio with a narrowed gaze, a furrow of concentration wrinkling his brow. Totally willing to let him figure it out, Andrea followed his gaze.

And saw a big yellow mutt corner Medusa.

"No," she yelled. Knowing her career didn't mean diddly if that dog went through with his naughty intentions, she ripped herself away from Percy and ran across the room. She'd call the cops and let them write a report; hell, she'd take out an ad in the paper admitting a dog in her care had been stolen. Just as long as that male didn't have his way with her charge.

She was through the door and across the lawn, when a loud ringing filled the air. Dogs yipped, growled and barked. Dog owners called for their pets, their tones varying from exasperated to scared.

"This is not a drill," Percy's voice yelled out from somewhere near the door. "I repeat, this fire alarm is not a drill. Everyone needs to exit the building now."

But instead of leaving, everyone freaked out.

People ran around like crazy. Dogs ran in opposite directions, either panicked themselves or thinking this was some kind of game. Andrea dodged bodies, both human and canine, as she sprinted toward the corner where she'd last seen Medusa and her would-be suitor.

Gone.

Heart racing, her breath coming in gasps, Andrea looked around frantically. Then she saw it. A tiny tuft of white-blond hair, knotted in the green leaves of low bush.

"Medusa? Here, puppy. Come to Andy, sweetie."

Andrea dropped to her knees, bending low to see under the foliage. Relief surged and she gave a long, grateful sigh.

"There you are, you poor thing. I'm here to take you home. Come to Andy, baby."

The dog looked furious. A breed that gave credence to the phrase "Beauty is in the eye of the beholder," Chinese Crested dogs were pretty much naked except for the long tufts of fur on the legs, tail and top of the head. Medusa, however, took that rare look to new levels since the hair spiraling off her head and ears was woven into long white dreadlocks, giving her the appearance of an inside-out spotted cat at a Grateful Dead concert.

"Oh, you poor baby," she crooned, reaching into the bushes to pick up the tiny shivering mass. As soon as her fingers were within biting distance, though, Medusa snapped, sharp white teeth giving a vicious warning.

Beady black eyes glared at Andrea with righteous fury.

"Oh, baby, did he treat you bad?" Andrea murmured, keeping her words low and soothing. Medusa was temperamental at the best of times. And this was clearly not her best. Andrea dug into her purse to find a bag of organic dog treats. She pulled out a few pieces and tossed them onto the lawn. No point in risking her fingers.

The dog gobbled up the kibble as if she was starving. Andrea kept crooning sweet nothings while Medusa was distracted with her hardened spinach, then slowly, as if approaching a live bomb, she reached for the dog.

Medusa gave a tiny growl out of the side of her mouth. Then, with a scary look in her dark eyes, she lifted her head so her wild locks slid to one side, and sniffed at Andrea's fingers.

Her heart pounding so loud she thought her eardrums would explode, Andrea held her breath. Even the friendliest dogs were unpredictable in stressful circumstances. And Medusa wasn't even close to friendly. Cringing and ready to yank her hand back at the first sight of tiny teeth, she waited. Medusa gave another low growl. Then, after a long, humanlike look of suspicion, she stretched out her neck and swiped her tongue over Andrea's knuckles.

"Good baby. Good Medusa," Andrea sang as she scooped one hand under the dog's warm belly, pulling her tight to her own chest. "That's my girl. You poor thing. Did the mean man scare you?"

Finally recognizing her rescuer, the dog started a licking marathon all over Andrea's face. Struggling to get to her feet with a handful of gratefully wriggling and licking canine gratitude, Andrea held Medusa tight and stood up. Looking around, she could see Percy guarding the exit through the throng of people crowded around the door.

Realizing she'd dropped her purse in her rush to get the dog, she bent over to grab it.

Before she could, she saw the goon through the clearing crowd. Crap. She'd been so worried about Medusa, she'd forgotten to worry about him.

Then he saw her.

Fury tightened his already angry face. Looking like a bull about to charge, he growled.

Run! She had to get the dog and get out of here.

She ran. Like the hounds of hell were after her, she moved the fastest she had ever moved in her life. The grass was slippery under her feet as she sped across it.

As soon as she cleared the exit, Percy slammed the door shut and locked it with a loud click. She had Medusa in the lobby. On the other side of the glass, a large, furious man looking like he wanted to kill them stood, shaking the handle and pounding on the door.

"C'mon," Percy said, grabbing her hand and pulling her toward the exit. "That won't hold him for long."

"Wait," she cried, trying to pull away and go back. "My purse is still back there. I've got to get it."

"Your purse, or the dog," Percy said, tugging at their entwined fingers to get her to hurry. "Which one do you want more?"

Andrea glanced back at the door. The guy's fist had shattered the glass so it looked like a spiderweb. He hit it again, making the wood frame crack. The few people left in the lobby stared in shock, then ran for the exit.

"Let's go," she decided, holding the dog tight under her arm like a shaking, growling football. "Let's go, fast."

6

Keeping an eye out behind them as they ran from the apartment building, Percy held tight to Andrea's hand, pulling her across the street.

Damn. That guy was huge. He'd busted the door frame in two hits. Despite his current sprint, Percy wasn't usually one to run from a fight. But protecting Andrea while fighting the same goon who'd tied her up and scared her…? As much as he wanted to introduce his fist to that guy's huge face, he knew Andrea's priority was getting the dog safely away.

As he yanked open the Vette's passenger door for her to dive into the car, he gave the apartment building a regretful look. He'd deal with the guy before this was over.

He'd make sure of it.

With that promise, he sprinted around the hood. As he yanked open his door, he saw the goon with fists the size of Texas come lumbering out of the apartment building. And looking seriously pissed. "Oops."

Jamming his key into the ignition, he peeled out as the guy shook his fist threateningly. Percy couldn't resist offering him a one-fingered wave of triumph as he turned the corner.

"Well, there ya go," he said, tapping his fingers on the

steering wheel to try to shake off some of the adrenaline still zinging through his body. "Got the dog, saved the day. Chalk another one up to success."

He glanced over to share a grin and see how Andrea had held up in the rush out of there. Before he could read her face, though, the dog on her lap caught his gaze. Holy shit. He did a double take. It was just as ugly at second glance.

"What the hell is that?"

Andrea cuddled the growling dog closer, rubbing her cheek over its hairless little face. The tiny body trembled against her. He could tell it was trembling because it was naked. As in, no hair. Just pink-and-black spotted skin.

Afraid he'd damage his car, Percy pulled over to the side of the road. With his forearm resting on the steering wheel, the loud rumble of the big block engine shaking the car in time with the dog's shivers, he turned to get a better look.

"That son of a bitch. What'd he do, shave it? We must've interrupted him before he could get the rest of it." Percy squinted, wondering what the dog had looked like with all its hair. "Maybe he was figuring it'd be a disguise or something. Like a rat."

"Medusa is a Chinese Crested," Andrea said stiffly. "This is what she's supposed to look like."

"Scary ugly?"

He understood Andrea's heated glare. But the dog's? Percy winced, pulling his sunglasses out of the center console to dim the impact. That was a turn-a-guy-to-stone glare coming out of those beady black eyes.

"Why's it giving me a dirty look?"

"You just insulted her. What'd you expect? Puppy love?"

"It's not like she can understand."

Andrea gave him a dismissive look, then turned her attention to the rat with wings for ears.

"Poor baby, she's been through such an ordeal," she crooned, her fingers rubbing between those bat-like ears until the dog quit its death stare. "You need to say something nice now to make her feel better."

"Something nice?" He'd have laughed, but Andrea looked serious. It wasn't that he didn't believe in talking to dogs. Hey, they were some of the best listeners he'd ever met. But this thing?

He gave the animal—he wasn't calling it a dog until someone showed him proof that it was one—another questioning glace. Long silky hair sprouted all around those big ole ears and off its legs like it was wearing ugly boots. It had a tail, and there was hair on that. But the top of its head looked like a mop. Instead of silky tufts, the long white hair was all bunched together in dreadlocks. Vintage Madonna meets Bob Marley.

"Well? You have to at least say hello to her. She's scared and needs to know you're not a threat," Andrea challenged. He switched his gaze to her, liking the look of her face a lot better. Then he noted the tightness around her eyes and the white tinge to her lips. She was scared. Some of that trembling was her fingers, he realized.

Damn. With a grimace, he gave the dog another look.

"Hi, Medusa," he said. Then, because he prided himself on being a man who knew how to charm the ladies, present company excepted, and because he hoped it'd score points with the now-glaring Andrea, he reached over to rub one finger between the dog's ears. "Aren't you a special girl. And look at that hair. I'll bet you wow them on your date Monday."

That was it. The best he could come up with.

The dog gave a low growl, then lifted its narrow nose to sniff at his hand. Andrea's quick inhalation, and the scary look in the dog's eyes, was all the warning he needed to know that this wasn't a good sign. But he'd run once already today. He wasn't letting a mouthful of tiny teeth scare him.

Even if they were accompanied by a glare that could turn a man to stone.

So, teeth gritted against the probable onslaught, Percy turned the quick rub between the dog's ears into a full-fledged pet. He even managed to hide his grimace when his fingers slipped from hair to naked skin.

Suddenly, the dog pulled back. Andrea gasped. Before either of them could move, the dog gave a flutter of its lashes, then licked its tongue over his finger.

"Hey," he crowed in triumph. "Check it out. I think she likes me."

The dog's licking turned to nibbles. The lashes fluttered faster. If Percy didn't know better, he'd swear the dog was flirting with him.

"Thank you for saving her," Andrea said, her smile as warm as her tone. Her eyes were wide with appreciation, and enough admiration to make his ego swell right along with other body parts. "I owe you."

"No," he said, intending to put that idea and the whole payment-for-services-rendered stupidity to rest. Before he could, though, the dog barked. Wriggling out of Andrea's arms, it perched both front feet on the console and nudged at Percy's shoulder with its nose.

"She really likes you," Andrea said, laughing. "I think you've found yet another female admirer."

"All the ladies love me."

Her laughter faded. Percy frowned. Suddenly, the energy between them wasn't sweet and flirty. It chilled, as if she'd pulled away without even moving.

"So, what do we do next?" she asked, lifting the dog back

into her lap, shushing it when it growled, and fiddling with her hair. All without meeting his gaze.

"Next?" Percy said absently, still trying to figure out what the hell he'd done to make her pull away from him. Again.

"Next. Do you have a plan?"

A plan? He barely had functioning brain cells, he was so confused. Frowning, he glanced in his rearview mirror. They weren't being followed yet, but they still needed to get out of this neighborhood as soon as possible. Then they'd figure out who was behind all this.

"We'll head back to your place," he decided. "You can settle the dog, then we'll decide what to do."

He took the jerk of her chin as acceptance. Starting to get pissed because he had no idea what had changed, or how to change it back, Percy finally shook his head, put the car back into gear and headed for the freeway.

Women. He'd thought he had them figured out, until he'd met Andrea. Why the hell was it that the one he wanted the most was the hardest to understand?

IT WAS ALMOST OVER, Andrea promised herself. Soon she'd be back at her sweet salon and this would all be over. She had no doubt that Percy would solve the case of whoever had masterminded Medusa's theft.

He was simply that good. At investigating. At kissing her crazy. And at making women fall all over themselves to get to him. At the time she'd agreed to his payment, all she'd been able to think about was being with him again. Tasting his warm skin, feeling his hard body move over hers. He made her feel things she'd only read about in books. He made her want to do things she'd always fantasized about. And he made her believe she was sexy enough for both.

But he made other women believe the same things.

Women much better suited for him than she was. If even for only one wild bout of incredible sex. Because what if it was only incredible for her? What if, as soon as he saw her naked, he realized he didn't want her that much? It wasn't as if that hadn't happened before. How many blind dates had her sisters sent her on with guys who, as soon as they saw her, decided they were only looking for a friend? Or a couple of guys who actually asked her out face-to-face decided after a naked romp or two that there just wasn't any chemistry.

Andrea blinked fast to clear the burning tears from her eyes. Sure, she wanted closure. Yes, she wanted sex with Percy, even if it was only one more time. But mostly she wanted more. And there was no way she could con herself into believing she had a chance of getting it.

Before she could come up with a way to break the deal, or even decide if she wanted to, Medusa struggled in her arms. Her eyes were fixed on Percy. The dog was panting as if he was a big bowl of ice water and she was hot and thirsty.

"We'll be home soon. Nobody else is going to chase you or grab you or scare you," Andrea promised the dog. "Calm down. I've got treats for you if you sit quietly."

The dog gave one last lurch toward Percy, then with a huff, sat her bony little butt flat on Andrea's lap.

"Good girl." Reaching down at her feet to find the bag of treats she'd tossed in her purse, Andrea gasped.

Her purse. She'd almost forgot.

"Wait. No! I can't go home," she cried out in panic, hugging Medusa protectively close. "That man has my purse. My purse with my wallet and address and cell phone and contacts and everything."

"Damn." Percy grimaced. "You told me that, didn't you? I was too worried about getting you out of there to pay attention."

Panic gripped a tight hold on Andrea's gut, making her want to throw up. "I can't go home. He's going to know where I live. He's got my address. My mom's address. Everything."

Her voice rose higher with each word, until the last came out in a squeak. Medusa, clearly having had enough drama for one day, put both tiny paws on Andrea's shoulder to stand on her hind legs and gave a tiny growl. To soften her demand, she swiped her little tongue across Andrea's chin.

Overwhelmed by it all—being tied to the chair, terror for her dogs, Percy showing up, the rescue and the chase, and most of all knowing that Percy could never be hers—Andrea lost that bit of control. Tears, hot and angry, slithered down her cheeks.

"No!" Percy shouted.

It was hard to tell who jumped higher, Andrea or Medusa. Shocked, they both stared at him as, still driving, he waved one hand in a frantic gesture. "No crying. Not in my car. Not in my presence. I can't handle tears. They make me feel like a big clueless doofus."

"I'm sorry," she said, her voice breaking. "I'm just—"

Before she could explain that she was feeling frustration more than anything else—at least, anything she was willing to admit—fueling her tears, Percy interrupted.

"No. I'll take care of things. I'll rebook my plane ticket and go sometime next week. Don't worry about that stupid deal, either. I'll protect you and the dog free of charge. You're the one who rescued her. I'll solve this case, get that perp behind bars and make sure you're safe before I go." Despite the reassurance in his tone, the look on his face still said panic. "But you have to stop crying. Now. Not another tear or I'll pull over and put you and that weird-looking dog-thing on the side of the road."

He wouldn't. Her heart swelling with a warmth that scared

her even more than the idea of the thug finding her again, Andrea knew Percy wouldn't abandon them. Still, she wiped her cheeks and sucked in a deep, cleansing breath to get control of herself. No point in making her hero uncomfortable.

"Thank you," she said as soon as she knew her voice wouldn't crack.

"Don't worry about it." He glanced in the rearview mirror again, then shot her a frown. "Here's the thing, though. He has your purse. If he has any brains, he has my license plate number. Which means we can't go to my place, either. We're going to have to hide."

"A hotel?" The idea of her, Percy and a hotel room held enormous appeal. Mostly enormous naked appeal.

"No. I don't think this guy has deep connections, but if he did, he could track my credit cards."

Worry once again smothered the fantasy in Andrea's imagination. Before she could ask what they were going to do, Percy told her.

"A friend of mine has a place in Pacifica. A condo overlooking the ocean. He's overseas for a month or two. I have an open invitation, so we'll go there. I'll make some calls. We'll figure this out."

"You really are a hero," she told him quietly, finally admitting aloud how much she admired him. "Thank you. For everything."

Percy just shrugged, as if saving her, her business and a dog worth almost as much as she owed on her house was no big deal. And to him, maybe it wasn't. Maybe it was all in a day's work.

But to her? It was everything.

Relief crashed through her like ocean waves, strong and intense. She was safe. Sighing, she leaned her head back against the leather headrest. As the warm sun beat down on her and the dog curled in her lap, she knew it would be so easy to fall in love with him. Because he was a hero. Because he always did the right thing. And, yes, because he was the sexiest and most incredible lover she'd ever imagined.

The question was, did she love herself enough to take that chance?

7

WITH A FRUSTRATED SIGH, Percy threw himself on the long leather couch and glared out the wide plate-glass window. The stunning view of the cliffs overlooking the Pacific did nothing to soothe his mood. It was as rough and gray as the ocean beyond.

Tossing aside the phone he'd just used to cancel his heal-his-life vacation, he tried to figure out what to do next. The smartest thing would be to leave Andrea here, safe, and head back to his office where he had access to his computer and his sanity.

The craziest thing would be to stay here with a woman who, while she ran hot and cold, only made him hot. He couldn't spend more than five minutes with her without the images of her body, naked, filling his mind and making him want to revisit every delicious inch of her. Sometimes she looked at him as if she'd enjoy that just as much as he would.

Other times, she looked at him the same way his mother used to when he'd bounced through the house with too much enthusiasm and broke one of her prized vases. With disappointed sadness and angry resignation.

With his mom, he knew he got that look because he'd been

a hyper kid who never seemed to remember the house rules. But with Andrea? What the hell had he done? He was a good guy. He treated women well. Damn well. Hell, he could offer up a list of references from women who'd swear that he was the best thing since fat-free cookies. Women usually loved him. And he loved them right back until it was time to say goodbye.

But Andrea? He hadn't clue one what he'd done to push her away before. Nor what put that distant look of disappointed resignation in her eyes just recently. But he'd bet money she'd shot him that same look just before she'd walked out, leaving him sleeping alone in bed with a satisfied smile and no clue that they were through.

He glanced toward the kitchen where she had scurried soon after they'd reached the condo. After borrowing his phone to check in with her assistant on the status of the other dogs in her charge, she'd claimed she had to feed Medusa. But she'd been in there awhile, and the dog—he was only using that term so as not to hurt Andrea's feelings—was sitting on the floor. Staring. At him.

It was seriously the freakiest thing he'd ever seen. And that was before Andrea had put a tiny pink monogrammed diaper on it. Because the dog was due to come into heat, Andrea had told him when he'd laughed. When she'd started to explain calendars and calculations and potential messes, he'd actually begged her to stop. She'd snickered all the way to the kitchen.

"Don't you want your dinner?" he muttered at it, wishing it'd stop with the obsessive stares. He was starting to feel like a cartoon steak waving in front of an animated lion with its ribs poking out.

As if that was the signal she'd been waiting for, the weird-looking animal jumped onto the couch with a graceful leap that sent her dreadlocks flying, one of them smacking Percy on the cheek. It planted its two front paws on his shoulder and stared. Just…stared.

Percy swallowed. The thing was only about a foot tall. It was naked, for crying out loud. With seriously bad hair. So why was it so intimidating?

"You should go see Andrea," he said, wanting to shoo it away, but afraid to hurt it. Small dogs were scary. All fragile and, well, girlie. This one, with its flirtatious looks, wild hairdo and nude body, was even girlier than most. Toss in an insane price tag and this was one animal he'd rather not mess with. "Go on, get your dinner. And put some clothes on."

The dog gave him another of those lash-sweeping looks, seemed to sigh, then climbed onto his lap and curled around three times before settling into a half naked, half furry, diapered ball. Percy stared in horror as if a ticking bomb had just landed on his crotch.

Uh-uh. No way.

"Andrea," he yelled.

The dog tucked its head into his side, its little chin resting on his belt.

"Andrea!"

She came running out, her hair flying behind her and her eyes filled with fright. "What? Is he here?"

Percy grimaced. He hadn't meant to scare her.

"No. Nothing to worry about." He glanced at his lap and cringed. Nothing much. "Can you get this, um, her off me? How long does it take to toss kibble in a bowl?"

With one hand still on her chest as if trying to calm a racing heart, Andrea took a deep breath, then glanced at the dog and smiled.

"I think she likes you." She took her sweet time crossing the room, but didn't take the dog. Whether it was because the animal was on his lap and she was afraid he'd jump her bones if her fingers brushed his thighs, or if it was simply to torture him, he didn't know. "And she doesn't eat kibble. Tonight's dinner is pâté. I had the pureed liver in a cooler in her bag, but had to steam carrots and broccoli and sauté the spinach to add to it."

Percy's mouth dropped. "That dog eats better than I do."

"Such is the life of a diva." Andrea laughed. "You should see her breakfast."

Unless he got to work on solving the case, he'd be seeing just that. While he had his own breakfast with Andrea. An amazingly appealing proposition.

Percy looked at Andrea. She'd either used her fingers or a brush she carried in the dog's bag, because her hair flowed like a silken curtain over her bare shoulders. The tempting curves of her body were softly highlighted by the cut of her dress, her shapely golden legs bare beneath the purple fabric. How bare? he wondered, eyeing the tiny straps holding up the bodice. Obviously unaware of his thoughts, her eyes gleamed with humor as she took in the sight of him and the dog. But it was the sweetness of her smile that grabbed him. Hooked him.

"So," he said after a few more seconds of silence, his voice low and husky.

"So?" she asked when he didn't continue.

"So why didn't you return my calls?" he asked casually. So off-the-cuff that it took a few seconds for her shoulders to stiffen as the import of his words sank in.

He wanted to ask why she'd left in the first place, but a man had his pride. Very little, apparently, but his ego was desperate to cling to something.

Andrea's eyes went wide, and she nibbled at her bottom lip in a way that made him want to beg.

Then she shook her head. "It doesn't matter," she said. "I

need to feed Medusa now. Not rehash something that just…
well, yeah. Doesn't matter."

He wanted to demand that she answer.

He wanted to say it mattered to him.

He wanted to beg her to give them a real chance instead
of always running away.

But all that would smack of desperation. And no matter
how desperate he felt, he'd be damned if he'd look it, too.

So he just shrugged. "So feed her."

Andrea arched her brow at his surly tone. But she didn't
say anything. Instead, she tried to kill him by leaning over
so the bodice of her dress gaped, showing him that yes, indeed, she was perky enough to go braless. Percy's mouth
went dry. His body stirred. Then she reached for his crotch.
He almost groaned.

Before she could touch him—oh, please, yes, touch him—
there was a low, rumbling growl. His lap vibrated. He glanced
down to see the dog, teeth bared, glaring at Andrea.

"Medusa, stop that," she ordered firmly. The dog growled
again, curling tighter into Percy's lap with her tiny claws.
Tiny claws that were, despite the heavy denim of his jeans,
too close to anything he wanted pierced.

"Hey, now," he said, scooping the dog up in one hand and
holding it out at arm's length. "None of that."

"Sorry," Andrea said, reaching out to take Medusa, who
growled again and tried to scramble her way up Percy's arm.
"I've never seen her like this. She's temperamental, of course.
But she's usually pretty sweet with me."

Sweet or not, she wasn't going to Andrea. Since he didn't
want her scrambling over his head, Percy set her on the floor
with a small thud.

"Go eat," he ordered.

The dog stopped growling. She looked at Andrea. Then she

looked at him. She fluttered her eyelashes again and with a swish of her long, sweeping tail and a toss of her dreadlocks, she turned and pranced toward the kitchen and her waiting gourmet dinner.

"Well, then," Andrea said with a baffled laugh. She stared at the open doorway to watch the dog sniff at the plain bowl. Medusa stepped back and glanced toward Percy, then gave a growl before digging in. "And she's even eating out of stoneware instead of Meissen. I'm impressed."

Gratified at her appreciation—finally something she admired about him—Percy preened a little, giving her his most charming smile before patting the leather cushion next to him in invitation.

Her gaze shifted from amused to intrigued, heat flaring in those gorgeous eyes. She wet her lips, glancing from him to the couch and back. Weighing the possibilities—which were obviously sexual. And the consequences—which only she had a clue to.

"You're surprisingly good with her," she said, buying time.

"The ladies, they all love me," he admitted.

It was like watching a switch flip. Her eyes went from flirty, sweet and considering to chilly and distant. Her shoulders stiffened, chin lifted and even though she didn't take a step backward, she might as well have.

What the hell?

"It must be so rough, being God's gift to women."

"Sure." Knowing he was dancing on quicksand but clueless which way to turn to keep from sinking, Percy hauled out his best weapon. Rolling to his feet, he gave her a long, intense look as he stepped closer. Close enough to feel her swift inhalation. Close enough to see her pupils dilate and her lips tremble. Close enough to smell the warm sunshine of her hair.

"Babe, they don't chase me because I disappoint them,"

he teased, reaching out to lift one long, silken curl between his fingers, then lift it to his lips. "And for you, I'd be the gift that keeps on giving. And giving. And giving."

Amused, Percy shared a teasing smile. Andrea didn't smile back. "So what's it like, having all those women chasing after you?"

Oooh. Irritated at himself for being so slow, Percy shook his head. She was jealous. She was so cute. He grinned, finally feeling hopeful.

"The chase is part of the fun," he assured her. "But if you want to catch me, I promise not to run."

If looks could kill, Percy was pretty sure he'd be dropping to the floor. He'd never felt as empty as he did when she stepped away from him. He hated to keep repeating himself, but what the hell?

Starting to get angry, Percy shoved his fists into his pockets. Arguing was no way into a woman's bed, he knew. Or, in this case, into her heart, since he wanted a whole lot more from Andrea than another bout of wild sex. Although he was having serious doubts about why at this very moment.

"Please," she said, crossing the room to glare out at the ocean. "You have no clue. You've never chased a woman in your life."

"That's bullshit," he snapped. "I chased you, didn't I?"

She spun from the window to shoot him a shocked stare, her eyes as round as her mouth. What?

"You did not."

"Sure I did. I asked you out, not the other way around. I called you. Even when you never called me back, I still called."

Her mouth opened and closed, but no words came out. She waved her hands in the air as if trying to find them, then finally shook her head.

"Twice. You called twice. Wow. What a chase. You must have worn yourself out. And that's after canceling half of our dates because you had to work. Was it hard to make the call between the other women, or did you have your pretty blonde secretary dial for you?"

"Hey, it's more than I've ever done before," Percy muttered.

Hunching his shoulders, he frowned. He'd only had Jolene place a call once. And, what? He was supposed to stop dating? She'd left him. If she'd stuck around, he'd have stopped, sure. But…

Damn.

She was right. He thought of the lengths that some women went to in chasing him and winced. He'd gone on with his life, only calling her because he couldn't get her out of his mind. But he hadn't gone to see her. He hadn't sent flowers. He hadn't said a word about his burgeoning feelings.

Because, what? He'd been worried about his feelings getting dented? So instead he'd stomped all over hers and left her believing he was blowing her off to see other women. Was that why she'd left? Because he'd made her feel as if she wasn't important?

Crossing the room, he was pleased that she didn't run. Sure, she stiffened, clamping her arms over her chest like a shield. But the brow she arched was in question, not in disdain.

"I'm sorry," he whispered, leaning in slowly, his eyes locked on hers. Her lashes fluttered. Her breath hitched, warming his lips. And she still didn't pull away. "I should have chased you. I should have let you know how much I wanted to see you again. To spend time with you."

It was like watching a statue come back to life. The stiffness in her face faded, the chill melted from her eyes. Her lips

trembled as they curved just a little. He could see the vulner-
ability now. Why hadn't he seen it before?

Needing to reassure her and only knowing one way, he
brushed his lips over hers. Soft. Sweet.

"Give me another chance."

He could read the doubt in her eyes. See the remnants of
the hurt he'd caused. A part of him, and not just the desperately hard part between his legs, wanted to push her. To entice her with kisses and distract her with the physical heat
between them. If he did that, though, she'd run again. It had
to be her choice.

He just wished she'd hurry up and make it.

She studied his face as if her life depended on it. Worrying
her bottom lip between her teeth, she finally heaved a deep
sigh. His heart sank. Still, she didn't say a word.

Instead, she reached out and twined her fingers through
his. Her eyes still locked on him, she led the way across the
room, back to the couch. But she didn't sit. She lifted her
arms, putting them around his neck so her fingers teased the
hair at his nape. Then, on tiptoe, she pressed kisses, first to his
throat, then his jaw, and finally—thank God—to his mouth.

Desire washed over Percy like a huge wave. Reveling in
it, he took the kiss from sweet to intense with a thrust of his
tongue. He was going to make this so damn good, she'd never
be able to resist him again. And just to make sure, he didn't
plan to let her go this time.

As they sank onto the couch, Andrea wondered when she'd
gone crazy. First, in letting Percy know how hurt she'd been
that he hadn't put any effort into chasing her. What was wrong
with her? Guys didn't like clingy, needy women. The only
way she could have come across any more clingy would be
if she'd attached herself to him like a spider monkey.

And then, because she clearly hadn't made enough mistakes already, what with kissing him every time his lips stood still and jumping at the chance to sleep with him in exchange for hero services, here she was. Throwing herself at him yet again.

Yep. She was crazy.

But as Percy's lips moved over hers, as his mouth swept her away on a wave of passion, she couldn't care.

Not didn't care. She wanted to. She really did. Her pride, her secret-held dream of being so important to someone that he'd risk everything for her, those things demanded she care.

His mouth trailed soft, sweet kisses over her cheek to her ear. His teeth nibbled, his breath warmed.

She melted.

Nope, she sighed, letting her head fall back against the smooth leather of the couch. She just couldn't care about anything but Percy and this wild feeling between them.

8

SHE WAS DELICIOUS. EVEN BETTER than he remembered. And considering how hot the fantasies were that he'd been nurturing from their single night together, *better* was pretty damn amazing.

His tongue trailed over the slender length of her throat, pausing for a second to bury his face in the sweet silk of her hair.

A part of him, the cautious part that usually kept him from getting shot, warned that he was already in too deep. Once had damn near ruined his life because he hadn't been able to stop obsessing over her. He'd spent three months fixated on her, fascinated with her glowing smile and clever wit. Sex, again, with Andrea might prove fatal to his heart.

But as her lips whispered over his, soft and sweet, he didn't give a damn. He'd pay the price, whatever it was. For however long. He just had to have her.

Completely giving in, and determined to make it worthwhile, Percy shifted to pull her sideways onto his lap. He took her lips again, sweeping his tongue along the lush fullness of her lower lip. Her moan shot through him like liquid Viagra, making the pressure of her butt against his rock-hard erection even more erotic.

His body strained, desperate. More desperate than he'd admit to anyone but himself, since he'd had a dismal lack of interest in other women since his night with Andrea.

Needing more, he forced himself to shift her off his lap. Percy stood, wincing when his dick protested painfully as he straightened.

"Why are you stopping?" she protested quietly, looking both innocent and beguiling as she stared up at him, her eyes filled with a need that made him feel about ten feet tall.

"I don't want your naked body sticking to the leather," he said with a wink. His mind racing with possibilities, he looked around and quickly found the answer. The faux-fur rug. He grabbed a handful of the dozen pillows neatly arranged along the fireplace and tossed them into the middle of the rug.

Hurrying back to Andrea, as if taking too long would give her time to change her mind, he scooped her up and carried her across the room.

"My hero," she teased, twining her fingers through his hair and giving him a warm smile. Then her gaze shifted to the wide windows where the sunset sky glimmered with streaks of purple and orange light. "Um, maybe we should shut the curtains…?"

"Nobody's out there," he promised with a laugh, carefully dropping her into the center of the bed of pillows. "And I want to make love with you as day turns to night, to see your body glowing in the evening light."

"But…" She winced, then gave him a look so nervous Percy wanted to scoop her up and promise her anything. "I'm a little shy about you seeing me naked."

He started to laugh that away. He'd seen her unclothed already. He'd kissed every inch of her naked body. Then it hit him. It'd been dark in his apartment. He'd intended to turn on the lights, but they'd never gotten around to it. And she'd been gone before he awoke the next morning.

Calling on a sensitivity he hadn't realized he had, desperately hoping it'd be enough, Percy took both her hands in his. He pressed gentle kisses over each knuckle. She sighed. He could feel the tension leave her body, bit by bit.

"I don't have the words to tell you how beautiful I think you are. Not ones that would do you justice. I'm not good at talking about that kind of thing," he admitted. "But you have to believe me when I say that I'm over-the-top crazy attracted to you, Andrea. To all of you. Your laughter and your wit. Your smile, your gorgeous face. And your body. I dream about your body."

Andrea met his gaze with a wide-eyed stare. He could see the same fear in those brown depths that he was feeling in his own heart.

"I guess we'll see how the dreams stack up to the reality," she said softly. Then, as if to prove her point and blow his mind all at the same time, she reached down and, wriggling just a little to free the fabric from under her hips, she pulled the purple cotton dress over her head and tossed it away.

The air left his lungs. His head buzzed as he took in the sight of her sitting on the mound of pillows, naked except for a tiny pair of pink lacy panties. He tried to swallow, but his mouth was as dry as the Sahara. And his body just as hot.

"You're incredible," he whispered, finally finding his voice. "Absolute perfection."

And she was. Andrea was, undoubtedly, the most beautiful woman he'd ever seen. And for right now—and just right now—she was all his.

So he'd better make the most of her.

With that in mind, he tossed his clothes off as fast as he

could. Straightening after kicking his jeans aside, he froze at the look on her face.

Awe. Her gaze ran over his body like a hot caress, leaving him flexing—everywhere—in response. Percy had never doubted his masculinity, nor his appeal to woman. But the look on Andrea's face almost made him feel like a god.

And he was about to take them both to heaven.

"Protection?" she asked all of a sudden, halting his body's swift descent. Damn. Percy straightened, looking around desperately to find his jeans. Grabbing them, he yanked out his wallet, digging inside to find a condom. Clichéd? Sure. But hey, clichés sometimes paid off.

Then, finally, he joined her. Unable to resist, he pulled her warm, silky body into his arms and held her against his. For a second, he buried his face in the curve of her neck and breathed in the floral spice of hair, letting the perfection of that moment wash over them.

Then he got down to the business of showing her how amazing he thought her body was. How beautiful she was.

His hands smoothed up her back, fingers tracing her spine as he brought her curves closer against the hard length of him. He pressed openmouthed kisses along her collarbone before slipping lower. With both hands, he cupped the gentle slope of her breasts, lifting them to his lips to taste.

Delicious.

His tongue laved her pebble-hard nipples. Her breath came faster now. Her fingers clenched his biceps, then slid down his waist. She scraped her nails gently down his hard, flat abs.

Then her fingers wrapped around the throbbing length of his aching dick.

Percy groaned.

His body throbbing threateningly, he knew he wasn't going

to last. He reached down, tracing the elastic band of Andrea's panties. His finger slipped inside to test her readiness.

And found a hot, wet welcome. He slid one finger along the swollen bud, feeling her tremble as her breath shifted. Her thighs clenched, trapping his hand. He shifted, sliding one finger. Swirling, then sliding. She cried out, arching her body against him, her hand clenched in his hair.

Still feasting at her breasts, first one then the other, Percy pushed her panties down. Andrea kicked them away, then wrapped her calf around his leg, pressing herself into his thigh.

Not wanting to stop, but knowing he had to if he didn't want to disappoint both of them, Percy's mouth left her breast. As he swiftly sheathed himself, he took in the sight of her. Brown hair splayed around her like a soft blanket and eyes blurry with passion. Her breasts glistened while the thatch of curls between her thighs beckoned.

He angled his body over hers and slowly, deliciously slowly, eased into her.

For months, he'd been telling himself that sex with Andrea couldn't possibly have been as incredible as he remembered. But as she arched her sleek, gorgeous body beneath his, her fingers digging into his shoulders and her breasts shivering with the power of her orgasm, he realized he'd been wrong.

Andrea was much, much better than he'd imagined.

She was his perfect woman, he admitted to himself.

Then, terrified by that thought, he gave in to his body's desperate demand and plunged deeper into her wet heat, losing himself in the incredible delight of her and losing his heart in the process.

OHMYGOD, OHMYGOD, OHMYGOD.

Andrea mentally chanted in time with her panting as Percy

took her on a sweet tour of heaven. Her body convulsed with yet another orgasm.

Her fingers dug into the hard planes of his hips as he plunged, each thrust pushing her closer and closer to something beyond a climax. Something she knew was there, just out of her reach. Beyond anything she'd ever felt before.

Then he shifted. He angled his head to take her nipple into his mouth. It was still wet and aching from the delight he'd already given it. She sighed with pleasure. His teeth grazed her flesh.

Stars exploded against the black velvet of her closed eyelids. She gave a throaty cry of pleasure as her body convulsed, clenching tightly around his dick as it plunged again. Once, twice, before he hesitated, stiffening.

Needing to see him, she forced her heavy lids open in time to see Percy throw his head back. His throat worked. The muscles of his shoulders and arms were rock hard as his hips pounded against hers one last time.

He growled, deep and low. She watched him go over, felt the contained explosion of his body in hers.

He was incredible.

He was amazing.

And for just this moment, he was hers.

Wrapping her legs around his hips, she pulled him tighter, grinding herself against him as if she could wring every last drop of pleasure from his body. He gave her a wicked smile, as if to say, Really?

Then he reached between their bodies to flick his finger along her swollen—and she'd thought spent—bud.

And sent her over the edge once again.

Andrea didn't know how long she lay there, her body still shaking with aftershocks. Percy's arms held her close, both absorbing the delight and reminding her of who deserved credit for causing them. Her heart tumbled over itself as she acknowledged that they were just as amazing together as she remembered. He made her feel beautiful. Incredible. Adored.

And most of all, worthy of being adored. Worthy of incredible sex. Beautiful enough to entice, satisfy and keep a man as perfectly wonderful as Percy.

But soon, as the perspiration dried on her skin and goose bumps erupted everywhere she wasn't pressed against Percy's warm body, her mind started racing. Chasing away that contented feeling of empowerment and leaving behind the usual doubts and worries. The paranoid, negative, worrying part of her brain woke up screaming, What were you thinking!

She shifted, trying to sink her abundant curves with their extra padding into the pillows beneath her. Trying to hide, in case he glanced down and discovered she wasn't a size five with perfect thighs and a flat washboard belly.

But he'd looked already.

He'd touched and tasted and worshipped his way over her body. In the light.

As if sensing her tumultuous inner argument, Percy's hand smoothed soft circles over her hip. He pressed her closer to the growing evidence that he was pretty close to being up for yet another round of sunset seduction.

He wouldn't do that if her body didn't give him pleasure. So why was she freaking out about it so much?

Without that voice jabbering in her head, telling her she was unworthy, she didn't quite know what to think. Should she reach down and see what she could do to speed things up? Did she get up and run away? Was she supposed to listen to her body and do it all over again a few dozen times?

It was completely up to her.

Talk about pressure.

With a deep, shuddering sigh, she decided to do the easiest thing. Listen to her heart, which was still racing from the intensity of that last wild orgasm.

And her heart said, for once, to give it a chance.

But that was the scariest thing in the world to do.

9

WRUNG DRY, EXHAUSTED AND exhilarated all at the same time, Percy forced himself to roll off Andrea's body so he didn't crush her. His heart still pounded at a machine-gun pace and he was pretty sure he'd caught a glimpse of heaven.

"Babe," he breathed. He intended to say more, but his brain function hadn't kicked in yet. Four times. In half as many hours. Not bad for thirty-two, he thought. Not that he deserved any credit. No, that all went to Andrea.

"You're incredible," he said, his fingers tangled in her hair.

Propping herself up on one elbow, Andrea smiled down at him, her face barely visible in the room lit only by the full moon.

"You're not so bad yourself," she teased. "I'd give you five stars for imagination, another five for execution and four for endurance."

"Hey, only four?"

"Well, we only did it four times," she protested with a giggle. "And the last three might not have happened if Medusa hadn't passed out from exhaustion in the other room. She's not used to so much upheaval."

Percy grinned. Clearly, he hadn't exhausted her enough.

He'd have to do something about that. His body whimpered. He'd do something about it later.

Before he could decide how much later, Andrea's gaze shifted. She stiffened, pulled away from him and grabbed the nearest piece of clothing, which happened to be his jeans, and held it against her nude body.

"What?" he asked, looking around to see what had triggered her shyness. Did his friend Kyle have a camera setup in this place he didn't know about?

"Medusa," she whispered. "She's watching us."

Percy squinted. He couldn't see anything. Jackknifing into a sitting position, he grabbed the remote off a low table and aimed it at the overhead lights. The ceiling fan came on, too. Leaving the fan on to stir the air, he hit the button twice to dim the glow. Enough light to see by, not so much it'd ruin the mood.

Then he saw what had bothered Andrea. And wished he was wearing pants himself.

The dog stood in the doorway, glaring at them. Her hair swayed around her as if it were alive. The animal's ribs were draped in speckled skin. She had that supermodel look of elegant starvation.

"Are you sure that's a dog? Why the hell did you shave it?"

"She's not shaved. She's a hairless breed."

"She has hair all over her head. Sort of. How's that hairless? Maybe if you comb out those dreads, you can cover her naked body with all that hair," he noted, seeing that the twisted strands reached the dog's shoulders.

With a tsking sound, Andrea yanked her dress over her head. Trying not to grin, Percy tucked her panties under the pillow. Sure, he couldn't see anything. But knowing she was running across the room commando was its own special thrill.

"Where are you going?" he asked.

"I want to call and check with the salon again. Just to make sure everything's okay. Then, I don't know about you, but I'm starving. I need to wash Medusa's bowl and give her her meds, and then I'll see if there's anything here for dinner."

Dinner. Percy lay back, his arms crossed behind his head, and grinned. Yeah, refueling sounded good to him.

A romantic dinner for two, maybe?

He wondered if Andrea would be willing to go out without her panties.

Enjoying the idea, Percy forced himself into a half-sitting position. Taking that as some kind of signal, the dog pranced over and pounced. Putting those reflexes he was so proud of to good use, Percy quickly grabbed a pillow and held it in front of his stuff just before the dog landed on his lap.

"Hey," he protested. "Don't you have somewhere else to be?"

The dog gave him a long, adoring look. Then she sniffed his chest, placed both tiny paws on his shoulder and stood. Wincing, he adjusted the pillow. She didn't weigh much, but still…

Then she started licking his face.

Percy snorted with laughter. He'd had women chase him before, but this was ridiculous.

"Nope," he said, gingerly lifting the dog away and setting her on the floor next to him. "I'm a one-woman man now, and I'm spoken for. Besides, sweetheart, you're really not my type."

As if she was considering his words, the dog tilted her head to one side and gave him a long, assessing look.

Eyeing her, and with unfamiliar shyness, still holding the pillow in front of his manly parts, Percy got to his feet to retrieve his jeans.

"Quit watching," he muttered to the dog when she started panting as he pulled on his pants. She ignored him.

He quickly yanked on his shirt but didn't bother with shoes or socks. It was only fair since Andrea didn't have panties.

"I'll make dinner," he heard himself offer as he entered the kitchen. Andrea, at the counter measuring out a teaspoon of some vile-looking oil, gave him a shocked look.

"What, I know how to cook," he said in mock indignation.

"You do?"

"I do. Nothing fancy, but enough to make you ask for seconds."

Crouching down and gesturing the dog over to her, Andrea gave him an arch look. "We're talking about food, right?"

"For now." He laughed then poked his head into the freezer. "Aha."

He pulled out a pair of chicken breasts. "It's a start. We're probably going to come up short on the veggies, but we'll double up on dessert to make up for it."

Andrea's giggle was sweet. He watched her give the little dog praise for taking her medicine like a good girl. She didn't seem like a food snob. Still… "You're not a lettuce pretender, are you?" he asked.

"Do I pretend to be salad?" she asked with a frown as she straightened, tugging her fingers through her hair, trying to comb out the tangles. Tangles put there by his lovemaking, he realized with a grin.

"No. Are you one of those gals who pretends to be willing to eat anything, but in reality, will only nibble on lettuce leaves and the occasional tomato wedge?"

Andrea's eyes widened and she gave a knowing nod. "Ah, my sisters are salad pretenders. They claim their svelte figures are gifts of nature, when the reality is that they live on undressed romaine and two hours of cardio a day."

"And you?"

"Do I look like a starved workout fanatic?" she asked, stepping back and holding her arms wide. His gaze traveled over her body, his mouth watering a little at the sight of her unbound breasts cupped by the vivid fabric. The skirt was loose and full, but he knew what was beneath it.

And, thinking of the tiny scrap of pink lace hidden in the living room, what wasn't.

"You look perfect," he said honestly. "You've got curves where a man likes curves, lots of smooth silky skin and a way of walking that gives a guy ideas."

Her smile was an appealing mixture of sassy and sweet. "What kind of ideas?"

Feeling much better about having dinner in the condo and all the dessert possibilities, Percy slowly approached Andrea, cupping her hips with both hands and slowly pulling her against the hard, welcoming length of his body.

"My first idea had to do with your mouth," he told her, trailing his index finger over the full cushion of her bottom lip. "I thought we'd start with a little kissing, maybe some nibbles."

Under his finger, Andrea's mouth curved in a laugh. "Nibbles, hmm?"

"What? You don't do nibbles?"

"I don't know. How, exactly, do you define nibbles?"

"It's more a 'show' than a 'tell' kind of definition," he said quietly, his body hardening against the softness of hers. He shifted his hips just a bit to keep her in the loop on how happy his body was to feel hers.

"I'm a big fan of learning," she said, her words a husky whisper as she pressed closer to his erection, shifting her thigh to rub against him.

Through with the teasing, Percy got down to defining. His

mouth slid over hers. Soft and wet, with just enough pressure to make her sigh. His tongue swept over the fullness, then he gently bit, offering tiny nibbling kisses as he sucked her lower lip into his mouth.

Her whimpering cry of pleasure went straight to his dick. Clearly, fifteen minutes was plenty of rest time, since his body was raring to go again.

But just when he thought she'd be willing to enjoy a little tabletop nookie, a sound intruded.

Low. Angry. A rumbling.

Percy tried to ignore it.

But Andrea apparently couldn't. She gave a regretful little moan, then with an ego-gratifying show of reluctance, pulled her mouth from his.

"I think she's jealous," Andrea said with a laugh as she studied the dog.

Percy gave the mutt a worried look. He was afraid Andrea was right. And he'd dealt with enough jealous females before to know he should be wary. Especially with this one.

"I'll cook dinner," he said again. He'd never cooked for a woman before. He'd never needed to. But as dorky as it sounded, he wanted to woo Andrea. "You go, take the dog and relax or something."

Mostly just take the dog. It was intimidating him.

"Do you think your friend would mind if I washed up?" Andrea asked, stepping out of his arms and running her fingers through her tangled hair. "I'd love to be a little more presentable before we eat."

"Sure. Check the guest room. He usually keeps stuff for company in there. You might even want to relax in the shower for a little while. After the day you've had, you deserve it."

Andrea paused in the doorway and gave him a teasing sort of look. With her hair tumbled in tangled curls over her shoulders and her lips still swollen from his kisses, she was pretty much the most tempting sight Percy had ever seen.

"Since you're making dinner, I'll provide dessert," she promised. The look she gave him made it pretty clear that dessert would include a side of naked.

10

PERFECT.

Percy leaned against the counter, grinning and wondering if there was any chocolate sauce in the apartment. Nothing like mixing chocolate with naked.

Enjoying the fantasy, he popped the chicken into the microwave to defrost and started scouring the pantry. He came across a bag of shortbread cookies. Grabbing a handful, he turned to see the dog. Staring. Again.

Percy glanced at his cookies. No chocolate. He broke off a piece and tossed it across the room. Medusa caught it midair and gulped it down as if she was starving. He tossed her another.

"You like that?" he asked.

The dog pranced over, did a twirly sort of dance that sent her dreadlocks flying in a circle. Then she ran her chilly little tongue over the top of his bare foot, as if in thanks.

He couldn't help it. It might be the weirdest-looking thing to ever be called a dog, but it was kinda cute. He grinned and, after a quick glance to make sure they were still alone, he bent down to rub his hand over the dog's head.

Okay, then. She looked happy enough to him.

Munching on cookies, and yes, sharing a tiny piece now and then, Percy started pulling together a meal. Pasta, jarred sauce and chicken. Good enough. He found a bottle of wine in the rack and opened it, setting it on the counter to breathe.

"That, you don't get," he told the dog.

She just fluttered her lashes at him as if to say she'd have some if she wanted.

Percy rolled his eyes, but before he could comment, his cell phone rang. Glancing at the display, he growled a little. Finally.

"You were supposed to stay at the office until closing," he said to Jolene in lieu of a greeting.

"You texted to say you weren't bringing in the dog, so I went home. I'm allowed to go home, you know."

"Right. But we close at five. I called earlier. A lot earlier. You weren't there."

Percy opened the fridge, looking for something to turn into a side dish. Kyle had emptied the fridge of perishables, so the pickings were slim.

"You're supposed to be on a plane," Jolene argued. "What difference does it make where I'm at if you're poking your toes into sand?"

Now, there was a euphemism. Percy snickered. Then, grabbing a bag of frozen green beans and a sealed package of bacon, he put a pot under the faucet to fill with water.

"My toes haven't seen the sand yet, thanks to you. This last-minute job made me miss the plane."

"You're not on vacation? No relaxation, no fruity drinks with umbrellas? Oh, Percy, I'm sorry. I made sure to get travel insurance, just in case. It was a little extra expense, but at least it's paid off. Do you want me to rebook the flight? When do you want to leave?"

Percy rolled his eyes. If Jolene were to be believed, he was as self-sufficient as a five-year-old and just as capable of taking care of himself.

"I'm fine. I don't know when I want to leave, so let's hold off on rebooking." Until he convinced Andrea to go with him, at least. "I have some other work for you to do, though. I need all the info you can get on the dog. What breeders are in the area, other groomers, especially one called Diamonds and Doggies. Besides money, what is this dog's draw and why would someone want it? Get me a background check on the Days, too, both of them. Go deep. I want to know their financials, why their marriage busted, where they are this weekend. Get me everything."

"Sure thing. I'll have it to you by tomorrow," she promised. Which was three times as fast as she'd usually pull it together. She clearly wanted Percy on vacation. "So what's the deal? Where's the dog? Did you retrieve it?"

"I've got it. But I'm not turning it over to Day until I know what's going on."

"If you have the dog, you really should return it. That's what you're being paid for."

"Someone snatched the dog and tied the groomer to a chair. Something is going on and I'm not handing the dog over until I know what that something is."

Cutting short Jolene's horrified exclamations, he told her he'd check in the next morning. It took another three minutes to assure her that he was taking proper care of himself. And of the dog.

Speaking of... Percy almost tripped as the tiny thing ran under and between his feet. Round and round it went, as if desperate for him to give it some attention.

"I've gotta get this cooked," he told her. "Chill."

She gave him an offended look, but chill she did. Curling into a ball of skin and fur by the refrigerator, she gave him another of those long, heartfelt looks, then went to sleep.

So other than being really, really smart, what made this dog so important that someone would break the law for it? Grumbling, Percy sautéed bacon to add to the green beans. All the while, his brain raced, considering and eliminating possibilities.

By the time Andrea came in, the table was ready. And Percy had a plan.

"Hungry?" Percy asked, not bothering to tone down what he was hungry for. Hey, she wasn't wearing panties. And he was damn near starving.

ANDREA STOPPED SHORT IN THE doorway, her breath catching at the look on his face. Talk about hunger. Her heart fluttered, dropping into a stomach already tight with desire. The entire time she'd been in the shower, all she'd been able to think about was Percy.

About kissing him. About tasting him. About drawing his body deep into hers, over and over again. Just the fantasy of it had gotten her hot and wet. Which was a problem, given that she had no idea where her underpants were.

At Percy's question, Medusa woke. Seeing Andrea, she gave a little yip and ran over for a hug. Laughing despite the fact that she was falling for the dog as much as the man— both out of her league—she swept the little body up for a hug. Medusa tilted that sweet head to one side and gave Andrea a look that said trust. And love.

Andrea's eyes filled, emotion clogging her throat. Here she'd been, totally focused on her wants and desires and issues. But she was supposed to be protecting the dog. They had to figure out why someone had kidnapped her and if she was still in danger.

The sooner they found out, the sooner everyone could get back to their regular lives. And the sooner she could see if Percy was going to be a part of hers.

She gently set the dog on the floor.

"Can we talk?" she asked Percy as she straightened, her smile closer to a grimace than a grin. The lust coiling low in her belly gave up the fight against the tension battling there for supremacy.

"Sure. Want to talk and eat?" he suggested, indicating the dining room. Medusa was totally on board with that, prancing around Andrea's feet before heading toward the dining room and back as if to say, Hurry up.

Andrea's smile softened, becoming easier and genuine as she watched the dog. She glanced at Percy, noticing that he was watching, too. Her heart sighed. Instead of bafflement or disdain, his look was pure affection.

"Thanks so much for putting dinner together," she said, trying to distract herself from falling too deeply for him. Not yet. Not until she was sure. "I'd offer to get groceries and make breakfast, but that creep has my wallet."

If that wasn't the perfect segue, she didn't know what was. Andrea stepped into the formal dining room and stopped short.

"Oh, my…"

Eyes wide, she took in the scene.

Candles of varying colors flickered on the sideboard. The table was set with gleaming white china, sparkling crystal and a pretty red free-form glass bowl in the center.

"Aren't you the romantic," she said, her voice catching in her throat. The part of her that didn't want to wrap her legs around his hips and squeeze him tight wanted to smack him. What was he doing, setting such a beautiful scene? Was he trying to break down every protective barrier she had?

"It's not much, but you should eat while the food is still warm," he said, indicating the covered dish.

"Thank you for going to so much trouble," she said quietly as she took her seat.

"So, you wanted to talk?" he reminded her as he dished up her plate, then his own.

"I was hoping we could figure out who's behind Medusa's kidnapping."

"Great minds," he said with a nod. "I was thinking about just that. So fill me in. When we went out, you were working in a salon, doing people's hair, right? What made you switch? Where do you find your clients? How'd you get Medusa?"

Andrea grinned at the rapid-fire questions. Glad to focus on the case, and on the delicious chicken dinner, she followed Percy's lead, talking and eating at the same time.

"Growing up, I spent so much time doing my sisters' hair, helping pretty them up for dates, that it seemed like a natural career choice. And I liked doing hair well enough, I guess. But when Viviana closed her shop, I realized I didn't love it enough to find another salon, or to even open my own. About a year ago, I agreed to do hair at a party for one of the Nob Hill bridge clubs. Before the night was over, I'd made over all six women plus their dogs. Turns out the dogs were more fun."

And they didn't judge her, or make comments about what a pretty face she had, then sigh as if pitying that the rest of her didn't measure up.

"And that made you shift from people to dogs?" Percy prompted. Not facts for the case, she realized. But because he was genuinely interested. Blushing a little, she glanced down at her plate a second to try to figure out why. Maybe it was the intensity of his focus on her. Or the fact that he'd seen her naked, really naked, and still wanted to know more about her. About her life. Wow.

"Um, it wasn't quite as simple as that, but from that party I ended up getting requests from the women to groom their dogs. It was a 'they told two friends, then they told two friends and so on' kind of thing. When I lost my job at the salon, and was looking for alternatives, I realized I was making the same amount of money as I'd been bringing in doing hair. So I spent some time studying, visited a dozen or so breeders to learn more about American Kennel Club requirements and grooming specifics, and interned at my vet's clinic to learn handling, health and hygiene."

"And then?" he asked when she paused to take a sip of her wine.

"And then I dived right in. The bulk of my clients are wealthy society matrons, but I've made some good contacts with breeders who appreciate that I use all-natural products and do more to work with the dogs than just give them a shampoo and set."

"You love it," Percy observed. "I don't remember you being anywhere near this enthusiastic before."

Andrea wrinkled her nose. Before, she'd been afraid to say too much and scare him away. Her momma always said men wanted girls who sat pretty and listened, not ones who yammered on all the time. And look at her now, sitting and yammering.

"I really love 'Fur'sace,'" she admitted. "Running my own business, calling the shots. The dogs are great, even if some of the owners are a little crazy. And I'm really good at what I'm doing."

"Was Eliza Day one of those early clients?"

And now they got to the case. Comfortable, and glad to finally start figuring it out, Andrea set her fork aside and leaned forward.

"No. I've only been working with Eliza and Medusa for

about two months. I probably told you before that my mom
and sisters have all married money—a few times. My mother
hosted a champagne brunch fundraiser and Eliza was there.
She and Medusa were wearing matching silk scarves and
flowers in their hair. The poor dog was allergic to the orchid
and had a rash starting to spread over her neck."

"Was Day worried?"

"Eliza?" Andrea laughed. "No, she was pissed. The red
splotches clashed with the scarf and was ruining the impres-
sion she wanted to make with her fancy, exclusive dog. That's
the kind of people the Days are. It's all about impressions.
I had some salve in the travel grooming kit in my car. Eliza
was so impressed, she claimed me as her very own groomer
from that moment on."

Still smiling at the memory, Andrea looked around to find
Medusa curled up at Percy's feet. Giving the dog an affectionate look, she said, "At this point, she's at my place three
days a week. Hair, skin care, general pampering. But mostly,
I think it's because Eliza gets bored with her, yet prides herself on being the perfect pet owner. This eases her conscience,
leaves her free to pursue her interests dog free and spends
her husband's money."

"Did she drop Medusa off today?"

"She rarely drops her off. Usually it's her assistant, or like
today, her driver." She saw the look of contempt on Percy's
face, and since she agreed, nodded. "I'm not saying she's a
nice woman. Or even a good person. But I don't believe she's
behind the dognapping attempt. There's just nothing in it for
her. It has to be her husband."

Percy made a noncommittal sound as he finished his
chicken. Then, after a sip of wine, he asked, "Tell me about
your competition. Who else is big in the dog-grooming
world?"

Andrea frowned. Did that mean he was dismissing her idea about Day?

"I don't have much," she said slowly, trying not to get irritated. "I told you about Diamonds and Doggies already. There are other groomers around, of course, but most don't cater to the rich and famous."

"And this Diamond place? They do?"

"Their focus is more on show dogs than spoiled lapdogs, I think. They seem to be doing really well. Raye's boutique is much fancier than mine and she recently expanded to offer pick-up and delivery services."

He gave a slow nod. Getting impatient because he wasn't even considering the most obvious suspect, Andrea frowned.

"What about Day? He's the one who has the most to gain by this. He'd be able to use the dog against Eliza in the divorce settlement. Or just take Medusa to punish his ex-wife."

Andrea was sure the culprit was Day. She'd met the man one time and he was an absolute jerk, exactly the kind of guy who'd hire a creep who wore a suit but no deodorant to kidnap a tiny dog.

"You think he'd hire me to pick the dog up after he'd hired someone else to steal it?" Percy didn't sound as if he doubted her. But he didn't sound as if he believed her, either.

"I certainly do. But you're the big detective man," she said, not wanting to believe he'd put money and connections over the truth. "Have you figured out who tried to steal Medusa? You know she's not going to be safe until this is solved."

Percy shifted, glancing down at the little dog now sprawled across his feet. He frowned at her, but Andrea still saw the look of indulgence on his face. Oh, yeah, Medusa was working her magic.

"I promise, the dog will be safe. I have a few ideas, but you're going to have to trust me. I don't like to make accusations without proof. That makes for sloppy detective work. You're good at your job," he told her, getting to his feet, "and I'm good at mine. I'm waiting for some info, but we should be able to settle this tomorrow."

Andrea believed him. Relief fought with disappointment. Tomorrow she could go home. There wouldn't be a creepy guy lurking outside her door, nor any threat to the dogs under her care. And maybe there'd be no more Percy. Sure, he was acting as though he wanted a future with her. Now. But would it last once the emergency was over?

It wasn't that she didn't have faith in him. It was that she had so little in her own appeal.

Which was a cop-out, she realized. She was sabotaging them before they even had a chance. She had right now. This was her shot at showing him why this thing—whatever it was growing into—should last.

"So what are we going to do with the rest of tonight, then?" she asked softly, taking his hand and letting him pull her to her feet. Their bodies brushed. Her breath caught.

He pulled her closer. Her breasts pressed against his chest, the pebbled tips tightening. Heat flamed low in her belly, fast and edgy with need.

"I did promise you dessert, after all," she said as his mouth descended.

"We'll figure something out," he promised just before his mouth took hers in a kiss sweeter than the richest chocolate.

11

HER BODY WEAK WITH PLEASURE and a lack of sleep brought on by hours and hours and more delicious hours of incredible loving, Andrea sighed. She wasn't ready to open her eyes yet.

She was even more unready for the best night of her life to end. But someone was licking her nose, and she didn't think it was Percy.

With a sigh, she pried open one eye and saw the tiny dog face surrounded by silky dreadlocks. The desperate look in those black eyes made it obvious what the early-morning wake-up call was all about.

So much for five more minutes or a morning quickie.

She reluctantly slipped out from under Percy's arm, glancing over her shoulder at him as she climbed from the bed. It was all she could do not to climb right back in. He looked so good. Lying on his stomach, his broadly muscled back was golden in the pale morning light. Tousled as much from her fingers as from sleep, his hair was a few shades darker than his skin. She'd spent hours tasting that skin. Caressing it. Reveling in the contrast of it against her own.

Before she could give in to the temptation to climb back into bed with him, she grabbed her wrinkled dress and, her nose scrunched in distaste, pulled it over her head. She gave the dog a "follow me" gesture and the two of them tiptoed out to the deck overlooking the ocean. Together, she and Medusa went down the steps toward the cliffs.

What a gorgeous morning. While Medusa sniffed around, Andrea stretched her arms overhead and sighed with pleasure, her body loose and lax after a night of good loving. The sound of the pounding surf and the warm morning sun filled her with contentment.

She was pretty sure she'd seen waffles in the freezer. Sure, they were a crime against great gourmet after-sex breakfast delights. But maybe with a little warm syrup or strawberry jam? Served naked? Yeah, she grinned. That'd work.

"C'mon, Medusa. It's breakfast time," she whispered, not wanting to yell and wake Percy. He'd worked hard all night and needed his rest. Especially since she wanted him hard at work again soon. She giggled then quietly slid open the glass door.

Halfway across the room, she heard Percy on the phone in the kitchen. So much for clever ways to wake him using only her tongue.

Then she heard what he was saying.

"How many times did you say Day called, looking for the dog? Really? Sounds like he's getting impatient. Did you tell him that impatience costs extra. Yeah? Well, I did exactly what he wanted, didn't I?"

Frowning, Andrea tucked Medusa closer against her. Who was he talking to? And what did he mean, cost extra? He wasn't working for Day anymore. Was he?

"Nah," he continued over the sound of clattering pans. "She's just a means to an end. Easy to use but just as easy to blow off later."

Andrea's entire body flushed hot, then flashed cold. She, who? Who was he using? Not her. He wouldn't do that.

"Right. I know, we have bills to pay. That's what this little hiatus was about, remember. Breathing room until I figured out whether I wanted the offer or not. But hey, if he wants to make me a rich man, I'm all for it." He paused, then laughed. "No worries. I promise, no woman could ever take your place. I'll never let you go."

Frozen in shock, Andrea could barely think. Through tear-blurred eyes, she stared at the expanse of white hallway until she pulled herself together.

Percy was using her.

He planned to turn Medusa over to Day, letting him get away with the dognapping.

And worst of all, Percy was committed to another woman.

How dare he? He pretended to want her, to be willing to commit to giving them a chance as a couple. And all the time, he'd just been using her?

Well, screw him.

Andrea wanted to storm in there and beat him over the head with the hot frying pan he was cooking with.

But she had Medusa to protect. Heart racing, Andrea realized she had to get the dog away before Percy went forward with whatever dirty little plan he'd concocted.

As quietly as possible, she tiptoed down the hallway. Scooping up Medusa's bag, she looked around. Other than her shoes and underwear, she had nothing else to take.

Her shoes were right there next to the couch, so Andrea grabbed them. But she hadn't seen her panties since Percy had slid them off her thighs the previous day.

"Hang on, let me see where Andrea is."

Her heart jumped. Pulse racing, she decided underwear

didn't matter. She had to get out of here. Before he came looking for her.

But after she was sure Medusa was safe?

Well, then she'd be back to beat him with that frying pan. She'd learned two things during her time with Percy. One, that heroes weren't always the good guys. And two, she was damn important and deserved to be treated that way. And nobody was going to use her then blow her off.

Deciding the front door would make too much noise, and besides, she was closer to the slider, Andrea ran for the back deck. She didn't pause to put her shoes on until she'd reached the bottom steps.

She looked around frantically. All she saw were the cliffs. Most of the neighboring houses were empty. She pressed a kiss to Medusa's head and blinked to try to clear the panicked haze from her gaze.

Concentrate, Andrea, she ordered. There was a hotel a couple of blocks over. She remembered passing it the night before. Deciding that was the safest, smartest option, she ran for the side of the house opposite the kitchen and its big windows.

"It'll be okay," she assured the dog. "I promise. I'll take care of you."

Just as she reached the front courtyard, a huge shadow fell over them. Looming there in all his huge, ugly glory was the dognapping goon. For a second, Andrea froze, terror holding her in its icy prison. No way. Not again.

Medusa growled. The low, vicious rumble acted as a key, freeing Andrea to run. So she did, turning on her heel and sprinting back toward the cliffs.

The goon was hot on her heels. He might be huge, but he was fast.

Faster than she was, she realized, glancing over her shoulder. There was no way she was going to get away. But she'd be damned if he was going to grab Medusa again. Desperate, a painful stitch in her side and her breath coming in hot pants, Andrea rounded the back of the house. Bright sunlight slammed her in the face, temporarily blinding her after the dim light between houses. Shading her eyes with one hand, she ran toward the bushes along the edge of the deck.

Another quick glance over her shoulder. He hadn't come through the side yard yet. Knowing it was a risk yet having to take it, she pressed a desperate kiss on the shivering dog's nose then stuffed her in the bushes.

"Stay," Andrea whispered. She gave the pooch a direct look, pointing her index finger to emphasize the command. "Stay, Medusa."

Shaking so hard, leaves fell from the bush, Medusa sat.

She gave a low, whimpering cry.

But she stayed.

After one last worried look, Andrea turned on her heel and ran toward the other side of the house. She kept her arms crossed in front of her, so from behind it looked as if she was carrying something. When footsteps hit the cliffs at the base of the deck, she ran even harder.

She still wasn't fast enough.

The thug caught up to her within seconds. He grabbed her by the hair, yanking her to a stop. Pain shooting through her like lightning, Andrea cried out in protest.

"Where's the mutt?" he growled, his fist wrapped around her hair. "You better tell me, or I'll make you sorry."

"WELL, I'M GLAD TO HEAR I'LL still have a job," Jolene said. "I was a little worried you'd replace me with some sweet young thing. And I gotta say, it'll be nice for you to focus on investigating and not worrying about bills and such," she continued, relief coming through the phone line loud and clear. Percy knew she depended on the income since her husband's retirement didn't cover much more than their living expenses.

"Now, what about this case? You're gonna confront these jerks, aren't you? Make all of them pay for terrorizing that poor girl and the dog," Jolene ordered.

She'd come through with the financial and background checks, confirming Percy's suspicions that Day's custody paperwork was fake. He'd have rather confirmed it after he and Andrea had celebrated the morning with a little loving. But they'd celebrate just fine after he told her.

And what they did after that was up to Andrea. She was his client now; she got to call the shots. He was reserving payback for what the thug had done to her for himself, though.

"I'll take care of everyone," he promised as he whipped egg substitute in a bowl for scrambling. He made a face at the concoction. Maybe if he added herbs and cheese, it would taste okay.

"And your vacation? Is that still on?"

Percy no longer felt that dragging negativity and loss of control that had prompted the desperate need for a vacation. Still, he wouldn't mind seeing Andrea in a bikini.

"Yeah. Next week for sure, and probably one more." He set the egg stuff aside and poked at the bacon to see if it was defrosted.

"You're going to be away from the agency that long?"

"I want the option of taking that long. I don't know how long I'll need to settle this issue." Or for Andrea to arrange time off. "You go ahead and take the two weeks off."

After a few more instructions, he finished the phone call.

Life was damn good.

Now that his suspicions were confirmed, he just had to brief Andrea and see how she wanted to handle the situation. Then she could go home and pack her bikini.

He hoped it was a red one.

Percy's body, still warm and naked from his phone-call-interrupted search for Andrea after waking alone, stirred at the thought of Andrea in a bikini, stretched out under the sun. He couldn't wait to rub oil all over her delicious body.

"Andrea?" he called.

Nothing. No response. Not even a bark from her canine shadow.

He checked the bedroom, but they weren't there.

Nor were they in the shower.

He'd heard her come back in from walking the dog. Where'd she go? He searched the condo, calling for both Andrea and the dog. It wasn't until he was out on the deck yelling and someone whistled that he remembered that he was buck naked.

He hurried back inside.

And noticed her shoes were gone. So was the dog's fancy bag. They'd been there when he'd got up to watch her and the dog play on the cliffs. So why'd she come in and get them?

Call him slow, but it actually took another search of the condo before it hit him. Percy froze in the kitchen doorway. Son of a bitch.

She'd left him?

Again?

Just like before.

Grinding his teeth, Percy stomped over and threw himself on the couch. Much like a pouty little brat, he acknowledged, whose fun toy had been taken away.

Leaning his head back against the cushion, he closed his eyes and sighed.

What the hell had happened? They were getting along great. The sex had been amazing. They'd laughed, they'd talked, they'd reached a level of intimacy that he hadn't realized existed. He beat his clenched fist against his bare thigh. And now she was gone?

Was this a test? Her way of checking to see if he'd really chase after her? His ego protested. He'd never chased anyone. His heart screamed to get off his ass and go get her.

Percy was halfway across the room when he spied the dog on the deck. Frantically jumping up against the glass door as if it had springs in its feet, the dog's weird hair was flying all over the place. Its tiny body was vibrating as it scratched desperately on the glass.

"Shit."

Percy sprinted across the room. He barely slid the door open when Medusa launched herself into his arms. Maybe she really did have springs in her feet.

"Hey, you're terrified, aren't you?" He tried to get a look at her face, but she kept burrowing her pointy nose into his neck and whimpering.

He cursed a blue streak. "Who the hell makes a dog whimper?"

Duh.

It was only because his arms were filled with a petrified, naked dog that Percy didn't smack himself in the forehead with the heel of his hand.

"The asshole found us."

Still shivering, Medusa pulled her snout from his throat, looked him in the face and gave a series of sharp yaps.

Confirmation?

Maybe she was as brilliant as Andrea claimed.

"Son of a bitch. Does he have Andrea?"

The dog barked again, scratching at his chest as if she was trying to make him hurry up and do something.

Since his chest was still bare, much like the rest of his body, there was an extra urgency to her plea.

"Wait here," he told her, setting her on the couch and running for his pants and shoes. He didn't make two steps before the dog was at his heels, yapping and running in circles around him, trying to herd him toward the front door.

"If I go like this, I'll get arrested. We can't rescue her if I'm being hauled away on indecent-exposure charges," he explained. Not bothering to look for his boxers, he yanked his jeans up, shoving his feet in his sneakers at the same time. He grabbed the dog, tucking it under his arm like a football.

"I can move faster than you," he told Medusa as he tore out the front door. "And fast is important. I'll be damned if that son of a bitch is going to hurt Andrea again."

12

PANIC CLUTCHED ITS GREASY FIST around Andrea's stomach. Her breath hitched and black spots danced frantically in front of her eyes. She should have run to Percy. Not away from him. What was she thinking, having to prove something?

All she'd proven was that her hair made a great leash and that she was an idiot.

Blinking fast to clear her vision, she tried to clear her mind, too. Girl safety one-oh-one, don't let them get you alone. His grip was too tight for her to move her head, so she could only scan the neighborhood as far as her eyes could roll.

To the left? Nobody.

To the right? Nobody.

There were only four condos on the block. She'd seen people on the cliffs, but that was so far away. If she screamed, would anyone hear? Not caring if she ended up bald, she pulled against the goon's grip.

"Where's the dog?" he repeated.

"Gone," Andrea gasped, trying to turn around. She'd rather struggle face-to-face. She might have a teensy chance of escaping then. And it would be a smidge less humiliating.

The goon let go of her hair, grabbing her shoulder and doing the turning for her.

"Where's your boyfriend? He got the dog?"

"He's gone. He and the dog are well away from you."

"His car's on the street, which means he's still here. Which condo? I want that dog. I promised my old lady, and I don't like to disappoint her." He pulled her closer, growling through clenched teeth to emphasize just how much he needed it. "So you better tell me where it is."

Andrea pressed her lips together and lifted her chin in defiance.

The guy's beady eyes rounded. Clearly, he wasn't used to being denied. He gave a slow, pitying shake of his head. Then he gripped her arms in both of his meaty hands and lifted her a foot higher, so she was eye to eye with his threatening glare.

"Where. Is. The. Dog?"

"Away from you," Andrea told him, her feet twitching in horror at being so far away from the ground.

God, how stupid was she?

She'd run away from the one person who could protect her. And why? Because she'd jumped to conclusions and listened to her self-doubts instead of trusting her instincts. Instincts that had demanded she believe in Percy. That she believe in herself. She'd used saving Medusa as her easy out, her excuse to run.

And look where that had got her.

"You'd better let me go," she warned. "My boyfriend is going to kick your ass if you don't."

"That pansy? I'll mop the sidewalk with his face if he gets in my way." Still, the guy loosened his grip, so she slid down, her feet gratefully gripping the ground again.

Now what? Did she scream until someone came running? Did she knee him in the groin and hope he wasn't as thick and stupid there as he was in the head? Escape options raced through her mind. She had about thirty seconds until it was too late, so she had to act fast.

Before she could decide what to do, though, her captor grunted. His eyes rolled back in his head and he heaved a sigh that washed over her like a tidal wave of bad breath.

Her eyes huge, her mouth probably just as rounded, Andrea watched him slowly crumple into a huge pile of passed-out goon.

"Oh, my…" Her shocked gaze rose. There, his shirt flapping open around that gorgeously muscled chest, was her hero. His hair was mussed, his jaw shadowed and the butt of the gun he'd used to hit the guy on the head loose in his hand. Totally macho, with Medusa cuddled in his arm like a ferocious baby, her hair flying around her like it was alive as she growled at the lump at their feet.

"C'mon," Percy said, his voice the same growling tone as Medusa's. "Let's go."

He grabbed her hand with his free one, dragging her toward his car. They raced for his Vette. Percy, clearly having not planned for a fast getaway, dug the keys out of his pocket even as he looked over his shoulder.

"Shit." He shoved the key into the lock, twisted, then yanked the door open. He pushed her in, barely giving her time for her butt to meet the leather before he thrust Medusa into her arms. "He's coming."

As Percy ran around the car, Andrea leaned over to pull up the old-fashioned lock on his door. He flew into the driver's seat and had the key starting the ignition before she'd cleared the console back to her own side.

"Go, go, go," she chanted, her seat belt clicking into place about the same time as the Corvette hit the main street. She wrapped one hand around Medusa while the other dug into the armrest.

"What are we doing?" she asked.

"Hang on." Using the car's Bluetooth, Percy punched a button on his cell.

"Yeah," answered a woman, her voice raspy through the car's speakers. She sounded like a two-pack-a-day geriatric with an attitude.

"Track me, call the cops. The bruiser is on our tail." Percy glanced in the rearview mirror, then read off a license plate number. Before the voice could respond, he disconnected.

"What's going on?" Andrea asked, turning in her seat to look at Percy. She'd rather watch his face than the road flying past. Actually, she'd rather watch his face than almost anything. Gratitude tangled with guilt, layering over overwhelming adoration at the sight of him. "How'd that guy find us?"

"I figure he found us through the dog's GPS tracker. We forgot the tracker was in your purse." Andrea winced, but he didn't seem to blame her. "That was my secretary, Jolene, on the phone. She's calling the cops, giving them our coordinates and his plate number. She'll call in a few favors so they hold him long enough for us to settle things."

That gravelly-voiced woman was his secretary? She didn't sound young and sexy. She sounded old and cranky.

Andrea knew the situation was serious since there was a creep with a head of steel chasing them. But all she could think of was Percy. Of finding a way to apologize, of trying to explain. Before she could figure out how, though, he continued.

"Or until his girlfriend, Raye Jensen, pays bail."

That got her full attention.

"Raye, of Diamonds and Doggies, is behind this? She tried to steal Medusa? Are you sure?"

"Yep. He's her live-in boyfriend."

Mouth open, Andrea twisted in her seat to look at the creep chasing them. "Him? I wouldn't have thought he was Raye's type. I wouldn't think he was anyone's type."

"Same address, couple of domestic-dispute calls with no charges filed but enough details to confirm he's her main squeeze."

Andrea tried to force her shocked brain to find a justifiable reason for the other woman to do something so despicable. She couldn't.

"So the Days are both innocent?" Andrea tried to reconcile that with her previous conviction that Gregory Day was a stone-cold asshole who wouldn't think twice about arranging to have a perfect stranger tied up and a tiny dog terrified.

"Oh, no," Percy said tightly. "They are both guilty as hell. But not of hiring our friend back there."

Andrea felt like an emotional yo-yo. Up, down, sideways and totally confused. Rubbing two fingers over her temple, she closed her eyes and took a deep breath. Then she looked at Percy and, with every bit of clarity she had, asked, "Huh?"

"That custody agreement Day provided when he hired me? It's falsified. Essentially, he was hiring me to do just what the goon did, but in a fancier way. Steal the dog. When I was on the phone with Jolene earlier, she gave me the lowdown. He's using the dog to get to his ex. He has no interest in keeping her, just in causing trouble."

Using her, then tossing her aside. Andrea's heart dropped. He hadn't been talking about tossing her aside. He'd been talking about Day tossing Medusa aside.

Andrea silently groaned. She'd jumped to conclusions, run from Percy again without explaining why and almost lost Medusa to that creep. All because she was so insecure, she assumed Percy couldn't possibly want to keep her.

Instead, he'd come after her.

He'd saved her and Medusa.

Andrea took a deep breath, trying to calm shaky nerves tying her stomach in knots. No more insecurities. From now on, she wasn't letting fear stand in the way of what she wanted.

And she wanted Percy. For good.

"Yeah, Day's a real prize," Percy continued, oblivious to the fact that Andrea had just overcome a major emotional hurdle and was going be making his life very interesting from now on.

"As for the ex," he continued, "I don't have her on anything specific. Except that six months ago she was photographed in the San Francisco Chronicle with Medusa and the Jensen woman. So they have a connection. I just need a little leverage to find out what it is."

Grateful for the reprieve from making any emotional overtures, Andrea forced herself to focus on the case. She wanted to ask what leverage, but at this point, he was doing at least eighty down a frontage road, the bruiser's Honda about a half mile back.

Suddenly, the sound of sirens filled the air. She turned in her seat to watch three police cars surround the Honda, forcing it to stop.

She gave a loud cheer and shared a grin with Percy.

"And that's our leverage," he said with a laugh, slowing down, then moving over to the side of the road. They watched until the cops had the guy in handcuffs, then Percy pulled out his cell phone.

"Make the call," he ordered whoever was on the other end. Then he tossed the phone on the console, gave Andrea a quick kiss that sent her stomach tumbling, fluffed Medusa's hair and took off again.

"Where are we going?" she asked once they hit the freeway and Percy's driving settled into a low rumble.

"To end this. Jolene's calling the Days to demand they meet us immediately."

Nerves replaced the triumph in her tummy. Ending things usually meant confrontations. She was really, really bad at those. But—she shot Percy a quick glance—she'd handle it.

"Good," she said decisively, lifting her chin despite the nerves. "I'm ready to settle..."

Her words trailed off as horror set in.

"What's wrong?"

Andrea tried to bury her burning cheeks in the dog's fur. But Medusa didn't have enough to hide the glow.

"Andrea?"

"I left my undies in the apartment," she muttered.

Percy burst into laughter.

Wrinkling her nose, she pulled her face out of the dog's fluff to give him a chiding look. "It's not funny."

"Sure it is. I left mine in the apartment, too."

Andrea had to slap a hand over her mouth to try to hold back the giggles. Then Percy grinned, giving her a wink. And she quit trying to hold back anything. Not the laughter, which rang through the car. Not the intense feelings she had for him, which were inching scarily close to the big *L*.

"Then I guess that makes us the perfect match," she said, putting herself out there like never before.

A part of her was terrified, worried that he didn't think they were a match, perfect or not. The rest of her was terrified he did.

Then Medusa gave her a look. Pure doggie approval. It froze the terror, so all Andrea felt was joy. Happy, falling in love joy.

PERCY GRINNED. WHAT DID IT SAY about the two of them roaring into a confrontation with one of the wealthiest men in northern California while neither of them was wearing underwear. Ballsy and cocky came to mind. But while he figured those labels fit him perfectly, they definitely didn't apply to Andrea.

He glanced over. She was murmuring endearments to Medusa, and giggling when the dog licked her nose in reply.

Sure, he was the big bad detective, used to taking risks. But Andrea had put everything that mattered to her on the line. Her career. Her reputation. For a dog.

His gaze fell on Medusa, now curled in ball, her black-and-white-speckled, hairless skin a vivid contrast to Andrea's purple dress.

Some things were worth fighting for.

Like women who knew what mattered.

THIRTY MINUTES LATER, PERCY pulled into the wide, sweeping driveway of the Day mansion and parked in front of one of the two portico columns leading to the atrium-style entry.

"I guess its confrontation time," Andrea said quietly.

"Not yet," he said. "I'm waiting to hear back from Jolene to see if she managed to leverage any info."

"Waiting," she murmured. "Waiting is good. It gives me time to say goodbye...."

Her words trailed off and she took a shaky breath before burying her face in the dog's hair. Percy frowned, realizing he didn't like the idea of splitting up the dog and Andrea again, either. Medusa's beady black eyes bored into him, intent and demanding. What she expected him to do, he had no idea.

Before he could figure it out, his phone chirped. He glanced at the text and grinned.

"We're good to go. If my plan works, we'll both be walking

away today with exactly what we want," he promised. He'd wait until later to tell her that what he wanted was, well, her.

Five minutes and a handful of dog treats later, the three of them were shown into the Days' parlor. Percy exchanged a grimace with Andrea as they stepped through the entry.

"Don't think we needed the escort," he murmured as the maid yelled, three times, to announce their presence.

The screaming couple in the middle of the room never acknowledged—or probably even heard—her. The woman gave Percy a shrug, rolled her eyes at Andrea then turned on her heel and left.

"Excuse me," Percy yelled.

The couple shut up. Both turned chilly glares at him. Then, after a stunned look, the blonde with the Botox addiction gave a high squeal and held out her arms.

"Snookie Bumpkins! Come to Momma," she called.

With a grimace, Andrea set Medusa on the floor. But instead of running to her mistress, the dog hurried around to hide behind Andrea's legs.

That set the snooty blonde off on another screaming fit.

Day strode forward, puffing out his chest and trying to look tough. "I assume you're here to return my property? A day late, I might add. Don't think you'll be receiving the full fee for such shoddy work."

"Work? Late?" Eliza turned her screeching on him, accusations bouncing between the two of them like a rubber ball.

Percy didn't blame the dog for wanting to hide.

"Actually," he interrupted coldly, "we're here to discuss the terms of the lawsuit."

That did it. Day and Eliza quit yelling so fast, you'd think someone dumped a bucket of ice water over their hot heads.

"Lawsuit?"

"What's he talking about?" Eliza asked, directing her question to Andrea.

"He's going to explain why he thinks we have grounds to sue both of you," Andrea explained. Percy knew he was grinning with pride, but dammit, he couldn't help it. She'd caught on instantly, without any coaching from him.

Smart. Sexy. Incredible in bed. And the sweetest thing he'd ever known. He'd bet she was a killer poker player, too.

She was the woman of his dreams.

"You have no grounds," Day snapped. His argument with his wife forgotten, he aligned himself shoulder to shoulder with her. The better to emanate that icy wall of disdain, Percy figured.

"I have very little," Percy agreed. "Except the minor fact that you hired me to pick up—or kidnap, if we want to get technical—a dog that didn't legally belong to you. I got ahold of a copy of your court order. You, Mr. Day, are not allowed near Medusa. So hiring me to go get her for you…? That was illegal."

The bull-shaped man glowered. His nipped-and-tucked almost-ex had plenty to say about that, though. All at the top of her lungs.

"And Andrea here?" Percy continued. "She's got plenty of reasons to sue," he said, turning to Eliza. "You promised Raye Jensen your business, and what? The patronage of a dozen of your best friends, wasn't it? If she'd help you with a little project to make your ex look bad."

"Tell them they are wrong, Gregory," the blonde demanded through stiff lips. "Tell them we won't tolerate this."

Gregory tried to tell them. He used big words, an intimidating tone and a lot of sweeping hand gestures. Percy let him go on for a while, right up until he noticed that Medusa, who was now hiding in Andrea's arms, was shaking. Poor thing. How often had she had to listen to this pompous blowhard?

Enough was enough. He and Andrea could play this out a little longer just for fun and drama. But the dog was already freaked out. She didn't need more stress.

"Actually, you're going to make recompense right now," he told them both with a chilly smile of his own. "I'll draw up the temporary contract for you to sign."

Looking around the room, he spied a pad and pen. With quick, easy strokes, he wrote up his demand. And added two lines for the Days to sign.

"Or else," he said, handing it to Gregory, who was glaring viciously.

"You know you're through, right," Day snapped, taking the paper but not looking at it. "I'll make sure you never get another high-paying job in this state. If possible, I'll have your license pulled."

"Yeah, yeah." Percy shrugged. "You go ahead and try that. Here's the thing, though. I'm willing to testify that you hired me to commit an illegal act. The cops picked up a big bruiser who kidnapped the dog and tied Andrea up. And it turns out, his girlfriend is willing to testify against Mrs. Day here, saying she put her up to it."

He pointed at the paper. Both Days signed with fast, furious strokes. Percy grabbed it as soon as the last letter was inked, tucking it into his pocket.

"So, you want to try and ruin me? Go for it," he challenged. Day's quick nod made it clear he'd be doing exactly that as soon as their asses cleared his front door.

"But if either one of you think, even for a second, about messing with Andrea or her company's rep? I'll make this entire fiasco public. I'll take you both down," Percy promised. "Nobody, but nobody, is gonna mess with her."

13

"FINE. NOW GIVE ME BACK MY dog," Eliza commanded in a voice shrill enough to shatter crystal. "You'll never touch her again."

Well, she'd been right. Confrontations sucked. And despite their clear victory, despair filled Andrea. Winning came at a price. In this case, the price was Medusa. Knowing she had no choice though she was miserable over it, Andrea lifted the tiny dog's head from its hiding place in her armpit.

"Bye, baby," she whispered, running a hand over Medusa's back, trying to soothe away the shakes. Both hers, and the dog's. Who knew she'd find it so easy to fall for a bad-tempered, demanding diva? The thought of never seeing Medusa again hurt like crazy. Her breath was a tight knot in her chest. Her throat ached with unshed tears.

"I can't do it," she said, handing Medusa to Percy. "I just can't."

With a tear-soaked kiss against Medusa's cold little nose, Andrea gave her one last pet, then turned and ran out of the room. By the time she'd reached the car, she was sobbing so hard, her chest hurt.

She didn't know how long she sat there waiting for Percy

to finish dealing with the Days. Five minutes or twenty, the misery was still fresh and cutting.

"Hey," Percy said quietly as he slid into the car next to her. "You okay?"

Andrea couldn't force words out, so she nodded instead, her swollen eyes fixed on a distant tree. She was grateful for his hand in hers.

Finally, knowing she looked like hell, but also knowing he wouldn't care, she turned to look at him. Her eyes didn't make it as far as his face, though.

Shock poured through her, quickly followed by joy and then worry.

"What…" She couldn't even find the words. Finally, her gaze met Percy's. "Why do you have Medusa? How did you get her out? They were both standing right there."

Medusa, wriggling in pleasure in his arms, stretched her nose high to give Percy's chin a quick swipe of her tongue. He grinned, then cast a cautious glance over his shoulder. Andrea followed his gaze. Gregory Day stood just inside the open front door, glaring daggers their way as he yelled into his phone.

"Here," Percy said, depositing the dog onto Andrea's lap. "We can talk while I drive."

So happy to have Medusa back in her arms, Andrea hugged the dog tight. She kept one eye on Day, though. As soon as Percy pulled out of the sweeping driveway, she demanded, "What's going on? Is he calling the cops? How'd you get Medusa out of there?"

"I carried her out. She likes me, you know. She jumped right into my arms." Calm and clearly satisfied, he drove the speed limit. Why wasn't he worried? His attention on the road as he turned onto the freeway, Percy handed her a piece of paper. "Check it out."

"Is this the agreement you made the Days sign? The one that will make sure they don't bad-mouth us, right?" She unfolded the note, her eyes rounding as she read it to the end. "Oh, my God. You got them to sign over ownership of Medusa?"

"Yep."

"I can't believe you did that," Andrea breathed in awe. "You forced them to give up a fortune."

"Yeah, well, you deserved something for all the crap they put you through." He gave the dog on her lap a doubtful look. "And Medusa deserves a safe home. With an owner who appreciates and loves her. Those two only see her as something to list on their asset sheets."

"I can see the threat of a lawsuit keeping them from bad-mouthing us," she said slowly, not wanting to rain on Percy's parade, but needing to be realistic. "But Eliza isn't going to let a piece of paper stop her from demanding the dog back."

"She doesn't want her." Percy nodded at her shocked look. "Seriously. When I mentioned that little flirtation in the dog yard when we rescued her, old lady Day was beside herself."

"Oh, my…" Andrea's eyes rounded. She knew Eliza would tolerate nothing less than a ranking pedigree to sire Medusa's puppies. But while due anytime, the little dog hadn't yet come into heat. So there really wasn't anything to worry about.

"Yeah." He grinned. "Her exact words were that she wouldn't tolerate a soiled flower. Then she ordered me to take the damaged goods out of her sight. Before Medusa and I hit the door, she was claiming that it was Day's fault the dog was worthless now and demanding he hand over their villa in Italy instead."

Andrea's face felt as if it was going to break in half, she was smiling so wide.

"For real? Medusa is mine?"

"They signed her over. I'll have my attorney contact them tomorrow about doing, well, whatever it is that's involved in changing dog ownership."

Andrea didn't know what to say. He'd done this for her. After she'd blown him off in favor of nurturing her neurotic fears. After she'd ruined the start of his vacation. And even after she'd sneaked out of the apartment without a word.

Was it any wonder she was in love with the guy?

"My hero. You totally came to my rescue," Andrea said with joy and admiration.

"I'd like to take credit, but it was really Medusa who rescued you this morning. She did the Lassie trick, running to get me. And you're the one who rescued the dog in the first place, remember? You and your handy-dandy GPS."

"Right," Andrea said with a grin. She really had kicked butt, hadn't she? Which made her the worthy mate of a hero. "But you rescued me from the heartache of saying goodbye to someone I love."

"All in a day's work, babe," he teased, sounding pleased.

And now she had to rescue herself from the heartache of another goodbye. One that would hurt even deeper. She looked at Medusa. The dog gave her an impatient sort of look, then crawled out of her lap, over the console and onto Percy's.

He didn't push her away. He didn't even complain about the discomfort of driving with her there. Instead, he gave her dreadlocks a quick rub, murmuring nonsense words.

Oh, no, she wasn't letting him go.

"So…" she said, not sure how to ask him for a date. Despite the great sex, maybe he wasn't looking for a long-term relationship. And she wouldn't settle for anything less. Not now that she'd realized she deserved the best. She deserved Percy.

Before she could figure out how to tell him that, she noticed where they were.

"What's up?" she asked when he pulled into the apartment building parking lot. "Are we here to get our things?"

Yay, her nerves cheered. Now she could put off asking him out. At least until they were inside, where she could persuade him with her wicked, naked wiles.

"SURE. WE NEED TO GET OUR things," Percy agreed. Although other than their underwear, he wasn't sure what they might have left in the condo. Still, both their places were a forty-five-minute drive away. And he couldn't wait that long. He needed to know why she'd left that morning. And what he had to do to make sure she never left again. "I figured we could settle Medusa down for a nap and maybe, you know…"

"You know?" Getting out of the car and hitching Medusa's bag over one shoulder while lifting the dog in her arms, Andrea's smile was as amused as it was naughty. He wished he could decipher the look in her eyes as easily, though. Was it joy? Excitement? And whatever it was, was it for him? Or because she had her dog?

"You know. Talk," Percy lied.

"Right. Talk."

Andrea laughed as she sauntered ahead of him to the door. She didn't look as if she'd object to some nonverbal conversation.

Back in the condo, he was too nervous to sit. Hands shoved in the front pockets of his jeans, he watched Andrea give Medusa water and a couple of treats. All worn-out, the hairless wonder offered a bark of thanks—or of good-night, Percy wasn't sure—then she trotted over to the pile of pillows on the floor. With one last bark, Medusa closed those intense eyes of hers and gave a puppy sigh before going to sleep.

Showtime, Percy told himself.

"Look," he said.

"You know," she said at the same time.

They both laughed. Andrea, giving the dog one last pat, straightened and came over to stand in front of Percy. There, just a few inches away from where he could touch her. His fingers itched. His body ached. He wanted her so much.

"Go ahead," she told him, pressing her hand against his chest as if to give him permission.

But she didn't take it away.

His ache intensified.

"Look," he continued, trying to find the words through the need and nerves battling it out in his brain. "Here's the thing. We're great together."

A soft, sweet smile curved her lips. Percy couldn't help it, he had to lean forward and kiss her. Just one, a quick brush of his mouth over hers.

"We are pretty good in bed," she agreed quietly, her fingers playing with the buttons on his shirt. But he could see it right there, her doubts. Sex wasn't enough. She'd left once—no, twice—because sex wasn't enough. And she was right. He hadn't put any effort into chasing her, into letting her know he wanted her in his life. So as much as he'd love nothing more than to give in to his body's urgings, he knew he needed to do this emotional thing first.

No matter how much it scared him.

"We're good at more than the lovemaking," he told her, brushing his fingers through her curls. Her eyes were red from crying. Her hair was tangled around her face. She didn't have a speck of makeup on and her dress looked about ready for the rag bag. And he'd never seen a woman more beautiful. Suddenly, his fear was gone. "We're good at the talking. And at supporting each other. We're a good team, and a good pair."

She bit her lip, then asked in a shaky tone, "Pair? Like a couple?"

"Yeah. I mean, I know you're busy with your business. And now you have a high-maintenance dog to take care of, too. But you're a smart, savvy woman. You can find a way to fit a little more into your life, right?"

"I am smart," she agreed slowly. "And I will be busy."

"Are you going to be too busy for a relationship?"

"I don't know," she said, her hand sliding down his chest, bared now that her nimble fingers had opened most of his buttons. "Are we talking a date now and then busy? Or..."

She stopped. Her eyes were huge and vulnerable.

Loving that he could, Percy came to her rescue.

"Or. Definitely or," he told her, sliding his hands around her waist to pull her close. "I want a commitment. A chance to see what kind of relationship we can build together."

"I want that, too." Her smile was pure delight. Then she took a deep breath and warned, "You should know something first, though."

"What?"

"I'm..." She bit her lip again, then sighed. "Well, I'm falling in love with you. So if we do this relationship thing, you need to know that I'm already in really deep. I don't know if that's what you're looking for."

Thrilled and more relieved than he wanted to admit, even to himself, Percy grinned. His hands gripping her waist, he lifted her up to meet his mouth.

The kiss was hot and fast, filled with promise and passion. But before he could let himself fall too hard, he pulled back and looked into her eyes.

"I've been falling in love with you since our second date," he confessed. "Crazy, obsessed, in love."

Her delighted laughter bounced off the walls. She hugged him tight. This time it was her mouth that met his, her tongue sweeping over his lips in a way that made him want to hurry this conversation along.

"Really?" she asked, a little breathless after the kiss.

"Really, really," he promised. He knew the promise encompassed a lot more than just assuring her that he was telling the truth. And he was ready for more.

A whole lot more.

"You realize we're perfect for each other," he said as he pressed feather-soft kisses along her bare shoulder.

"Perfect," she agreed breathlessly, her hands skimming an enticing trail down his belly. When her fingers hit the snap of his jeans, Percy pulled back and gave her a big smile.

"Yep. Perfect. I mean, we like the same things. We're crazy about the same dog. We have some very serious feelings going for each other." Then he paused, his fingers gathering the fabric of her dress, pulling it higher and higher until he could feel her soft flesh.

"And neither one of us is wearing any underwear."

* * * * *

PASSION

COMING NEXT MONTH
AVAILABLE JUNE 26, 2012

#693 LEAD ME HOME
Sons of Chance
Vicki Lewis Thompson

Matthew Tredway has made a name for himself as a world-class horse trainer. Only, after one night with Aurelia Smith, he's the one being led around by the nose....

#694 THE GUY MOST LIKELY TO...
A Blazing Hot Summer Read
Leslie Kelly, Janelle Denison and Julie Leto

Every school has one. That special guy, the one every girl had to have or they'd just die! Did you ever wonder what happened to him? Come back to school with three of Blaze's bestselling authors and find out how great the nights are after the glory days are over....

#695 TALL, DARK & RECKLESS
Heather MacAllister

After interviewing a thousand men, dating coach Piper Scott knows handsome daredevil foreign journalist Mark Banning is definitely not her type—but what if he's her perfect man?

#696 NO HOLDS BARRED
Forbidden Fantasies
Cara Summers

Defense attorney Piper MacPherson is being threatened by a stalker and protected by FBI profiler Duncan Sutherland. Her problem? She's not sure which is more dangerous....

#697 BREATHLESS ON THE BEACH
Flirting with Justice
Wendy Etherington

When PR exec Victoria Holmes attends a client's beach-house party, she has no idea there'll be cowboys—well, one cowboy. Lucky for Victoria, Jarred McKenna's not afraid to get a little wet....

#698 NO GOING BACK
Uniformly Hot!
Karen Foley

Army Special Ops commando Chase Rawlins has been trained to handle anything. Only, little does he guess how much he'll enjoy "handling" sexy publicist Kate Fitzgerald!

You can find more information on upcoming Harlequin®
titles, free excerpts and more at www.Harlequin.com.

HBCNM0612

REQUEST YOUR FREE BOOKS!
2 FREE NOVELS PLUS 2 FREE GIFTS!

red-hot reads!

YES! Please send me 2 FREE Harlequin® Blaze™ novels and my 2 FREE gifts (gifts are worth about $10). After receiving them, if I don't wish to receive any more books, I can return the shipping statement marked "cancel." If I don't cancel, I will receive 6 brand-new novels every month and be billed just $4.49 per book in the U.S. or $4.96 per book in Canada. That's a saving of at least 14% off the cover price. It's quite a bargain. Shipping and handling is just 50¢ per book in the U.S. and 75¢ per book in Canada.* I understand that accepting the 2 free books and gifts places me under no obligation to buy anything. I can always return a shipment and cancel at any time. Even if I never buy another book, the two free books and gifts are mine to keep forever.

151/351 HDN FEQE

Name	(PLEASE PRINT)	
Address		Apt. #
City	State/Prov.	Zip/Postal Code

Signature (if under 18, a parent or guardian must sign)

Mail to the **Reader Service:**
IN U.S.A.: P.O. Box 1867, Buffalo, NY 14240-1867
IN CANADA: P.O. Box 609, Fort Erie, Ontario L2A 5X3

Not valid for current subscribers to Harlequin Blaze books.

Want to try two free books from another line?
Call 1-800-873-8635 or visit www.ReaderService.com.

* Terms and prices subject to change without notice. Prices do not include applicable taxes. Sales tax applicable in N.Y. Canadian residents will be charged applicable taxes. Offer not valid in Quebec. This offer is limited to one order per household. All orders subject to credit approval. Credit or debit balances in a customer's account(s) may be offset by any other outstanding balance owed by or to the customer. Please allow 4 to 6 weeks for delivery. Offer available while quantities last.

Your Privacy—The Reader Service is committed to protecting your privacy. Our Privacy Policy is available online at www.ReaderService.com or upon request from the Reader Service.

We make a portion of our mailing list available to reputable third parties that offer products we believe may interest you. If you prefer that we not exchange your name with third parties, or if you wish to clarify or modify your communication preferences, please visit us at www.ReaderService.com/consumerchoice or write to us at Reader Service Preference Service, P.O. Box 9062, Buffalo, NY 14269. Include your complete name and address.

HBI1B

New York Times *and* USA TODAY *bestselling author Vicki Lewis Thompson returns with yet another irresistible cowpoke! Meet Mathew Tredway—cowboy, horse whisperer and honorary Son of Chance.*

Read on for a sneak peek from the bestselling miniseries SONS OF CHANCE:

LEAD ME HOME *Available July 2012 only from Harlequin® Blaze™.*

AS MATTHEW RETURNED to the corral and Houdini, the taste of Aurelia's mouth was on his lips and her scent clung to his clothes. He'd briefly satisfied the craving growing within him, and like a light snack before a meal, it would have to do.

When he'd first walked into the kitchen, his mind had been occupied with the challenge of training Houdini. He'd thought his concentration would hold long enough to get some carrots, ask about the corn bread and leave before succumbing to Aurelia's appeal. He'd miscalculated. Within a very short time, desire had claimed every brain cell.

Although seducing her this morning was out of the question, his libido had demanded some sort of satisfaction. He'd tried to deny that urge and had nearly made it out of the house. Apparently his willpower was no match for the temptation of Aurelia's mouth, though, and he'd turned around.

If he'd ever felt this kind of desperate need for a woman, he couldn't recall it. During the night, as he'd lain in his narrow bunk listening to the cowhands snore, he'd searched for an explanation as to why Aurelia affected him this way. Sometime in the early-morning hours he'd come up with the answer. After years of dating women who were rolling stones like he was, he'd developed an itch for a hearth-and-home kind of woman. Aurelia, with her cooking skills and voluptuous body, could give him that.

With luck, once he'd scratched this particular itch, he'd be fine again. He certainly hoped so, because he had no intention of giving up his career, and travel was a built-in requirement. Plus he liked to travel and had no real desire to stay in one spot and become domesticated.

Tonight he'd say all that to Aurelia, because he didn't want her going into this with any illusions about permanence. He figured that when the right guy came along, she'd get married and have kids.

Too bad that guy wouldn't be him….

Will Aurelia be the one to corral this cowboy for good?
Find out in: LEAD ME HOME

Available July 2012
wherever Harlequin® Blaze™ books are sold.

This summer, celebrate everything Western
with Harlequin® Books!
www.Harlequin.com/Western

Harlequin *Blaze*™

red-hot reads

Three men dare to live up to naughty reputations....

Leslie Kelly

Janelle Denison and Julie Leto

bring you a collection of steamy stories in

THE GUY MOST LIKELY TO...

Underneath It All

When Seth Crowder goes back for his ten-year high school reunion, he's hoping he'll finally get a chance with the one girl he ever loved. Lauren DeSantos has convinced herself she is over him...but Seth isn't going to let her walk away again.

Can't Get You Out of My Head

In high school, cheerleader Ali Seaver had the hots for computer nerd Will Beckman but stayed away in fear of her reputation. Now, ten years later, she's ready to take a chance and go for what she's always wanted.

A Moment Like This

For successful party planner Erica Holt, organizing her high school reunion provides no challenge—until sexy Scott Ripley checks "yes" on his RSVP, revving Erica's sex drive to its peak.

Available July wherever books are sold.